The Temptation of St. Antony
A Revelation of the Soul

Gustave Flaubert

The Temptation of St. Antony: A Revelation of the Soul

The present edition is a reproduction of previous publication of this classic work. Minor typographical errors may have been corrected without note; however, for an authentic reading experience the spelling, punctuation, and capitalization have been retained from the original text.

ISBN: 978-1-63637-491-8

CONTENTS

CHAPTER I

A Holy Saint

IT is in the Thebaïd, on the heights of a mountain, where a platform, shaped like a crescent, is surrounded by huge stones.

The Hermit's cell occupies the background. It is built of mud and reeds, flat-roofed and doorless. Inside are seen a pitcher and a loaf of black bread; in the centre, on a wooden support, a large book; on the ground, here and there, bits of rush-work, a mat or two, a basket and a knife.

Some ten paces or so from the cell a tall cross is planted in the ground; and, at the other end of the platform, a gnarled old palm-tree leans over the abyss, for the side of the mountain is scarped; and at the bottom of the cliff the Nile swells, as it were, into a lake.

To right and left, the view is bounded by the enclosing rocks; but, on the side of the desert, immense undulations of a yellowish ash-colour rise, one above and one beyond the other, like the lines of a sea-coast; while, far off, beyond the sands, the mountains of the Libyan range form a wall of chalk-like whiteness faintly shaded with violet haze. In front, the sun is going down. Towards the north, the sky has a pearl-grey tint; while, at the zenith, purple clouds, like the tufts of a gigantic mane, stretch over the blue vault. These purple streaks grow browner; the patches of blue assume the paleness of mother-of-pearl. The bushes, the pebbles, the earth, now wear the hard colour of bronze, and through space floats a golden dust so fine that it is scarcely distinguishable from the vibrations of light.

Saint Antony, who has a long beard, unshorn locks, and a tunic of goatskin, is seated, cross-legged, engaged in making mats. No sooner has the sun disappeared than he heaves a deep sigh, and gazing towards the horizon:

"Another day! Another day gone! I was not so miserable in former times as I am now! Before the night was over, I used to begin my prayers; then I would go down to the river to fetch water, and would reascend the rough mountain pathway, singing a hymn, with the water-bottle on my shoulder. After that, I used to amuse myself by arranging everything in my cell. I used to take up my tools, and examine the mats, to see whether they were evenly cut, and the baskets, to see whether they were light; for it seemed to me then that even my most trifling acts were duties which I performed with ease. At regulated hours I left off my work and prayed, with my two arms extended. I felt as if a fountain of mercy were flowing from Heaven above into my heart. But now it is dried up. Why is this? ..."

He proceeds slowly into the rocky enclosure.

"When I left home, everyone found fault with me. My mother sank into a dying state; my sister, from a distance, made signs to me to come back; and the other one wept, Ammonaria, that child whom I used to meet every evening, beside the cistern, as she was leading away her cattle. She ran after me. The rings on her feet glittered in the dust, and her tunic, open at the hips, fluttered in the wind. The old ascetic who hurried me from the spot addressed her, as we fled, in loud and menacing tones. Then our two camels kept galloping continuously, till at length every familiar object had vanished from my sight.

"At first, I selected for my abode the tomb of one of the Pharaohs. But some enchantment surrounds those subterranean palaces, amid whose gloom the air is stifled with the decayed odour of aromatics. From the depths of the sarcophagi I heard a mournful voice arise, that called me by name—or rather, as it seemed to me, all the fearful pictures on the walls started into hideous life. Then I fled to the borders of the Red Sea into a citadel in ruins. There I had for companions the scorpions that crawled amongst the stones, and, overhead, the eagles who were continually whirling across the azure sky. At night, I was torn by talons, bitten by beaks, or brushed with light wings; and horrible demons, yelling in my ears, hurled me to the earth. At last, the drivers of a caravan, which was journeying towards Alexandria, rescued me, and carried me along with them.

"After this, I became a pupil of the venerable Didymus. Though he was blind, no one equalled him in knowledge of the Scriptures. When our lesson was ended, he used to take my arm, and, with my aid, ascend the Panium, from whose summit could be seen the Pharos and the open sea. Then we would return home, passing along the quays, where we brushed against men of every nation, including the Cimmerians, clad in bearskin, and the Gymnosophists of the Ganges, who smear their bodies with cow-dung. There were continual conflicts in the streets, some of which were caused by the Jews' refusal to pay taxes, and others by the attempts of the seditious to drive out the Romans. Besides, the city is filled with heretics, the followers of Manes, of Valentinus, of Basilides, and of Arius, all of them eagerly striving to discuss with you points of doctrine and to convert you to their views.

"Their discourses sometimes come back to my memory; and, though I try not to dwell upon them, they haunt my thoughts.

"I next took refuge in Colzin, and, when I had undergone a severe penance, I no longer feared the wrath of God. Many persons gathered around me, offering to become anchorites. I imposed on them a rule of life in antagonism to the vagaries of Gnosticism and the sophistries of the philosophers. Communications now reached me from every quarter, and people came a great distance to see me.

"Meanwhile, the populace continued to torture the confessors; and I was led back to Alexandria by an ardent thirst for martyrdom. I found on my arrival that the persecution had ceased three days before. Just as I was returning, my path was blocked by a great crowd in front of the Temple of Serapis. I was told that the Governor was about to make one final example. In the centre of the portico, in the broad light of day, a naked woman was fastened to a pillar, while two soldiers were scourging her. At each stroke her entire frame writhed. Suddenly, she cast a wild look around, her trembling lips parted; and, above the heads of the multitude, her figure wrapped, as it were, in her flowing hair, methought I recognised Ammonaria. ... Yet this one was taller—and beautiful, exceedingly!"

He draws his hand across his brow.

"No! no! I must not think upon it!

"On another occasion, Athanasius asked me to assist him against the Arians. At that time, they had confined themselves to attacking him with invectives and ridicule. Since then, however, he has been calumniated, deprived of his see, and banished. Where is he now? I know not! People concern themselves so little about bringing me any news! All my disciples have abandoned me, Hilarion like the rest.

"He was, perhaps, fifteen years of age when he came to me, and his mind was so much filled with curiosity that every moment he was asking me questions. Then he would listen with a pensive air; and, without a murmur, he would run to fetch whatever I wanted— more nimble than a kid, and gay enough, moreover, to make even a patriarch laugh. He was a son to me!"

The sky is red; the earth completely dark. Agitated by the wind, clouds of sand rise, like winding-sheets, and then fall again. All at once, in a clear space in the heavens, a flock of birds flits by, forming a kind of triangular battalion, resembling a piece of metal with its edges alone vibrating.

Antony glances at them.

"Ah! how I should like to follow them! How often, too, have I not wistfully gazed at the long boats with their sails resembling wings, especially when they bore away those who had been my guests! What happy times I used to have with them! What outpourings! None of them interested me more than Ammon. He described to me his journey to Rome, the Catacombs, the Coliseum, the piety of illustrious women, and a thousand other things. And yet I was

4

unwilling to go away with him! How came I to be so obstinate in clinging to this solitary life? It might have been better for me had I stayed with the monks of Nitria when they besought me to do so. They occupy separate cells, and yet communicate with one another. On Sunday the trumpet calls them to the church, where you may see three whips hung up, which are reserved for the punishment of thieves and intruders, for they maintain very severe discipline.

"Nevertheless, they do not stand in need of gifts, for the faithful bring them eggs, fruit, and even instruments for removing thorns from their feet. There are vineyards around Pisperi, and those of Pabenum have a raft, in which they go forth to seek provisions.

"But I should have served my brethren more effectually by being a simple priest. I might succour the poor, administer the sacraments, and guard the purity of domestic life. Besides, all the laity are not lost, and there was nothing to prevent me from being, for example, a grammarian or a philosopher. I should have had in my room a sphere made of reeds, tablets always in my hand, young people around me, and a crown of laurel suspended as an emblem over my door.

"But there is too much pride in such triumphs! Better be a soldier. I was strong and courageous enough to manage engines of war, to traverse gloomy forests, or, with helmet on head, to enter smoking cities. More than this, there would be nothing to hinder me from purchasing with my earnings the office of toll-keeper of some bridge, and travellers would relate to me their histories, pointing out to me heaps of curious objects which they had stowed away in their baggage.

"On festival days the merchants of Alexandria sail along the Canopic branch of the Nile and drink wine from cups of lotus, to the sound of tambourines, which make all the taverns near the river shake. Beyond, trees, cut cone-fashion, protect the peaceful farmsteads against the south wind. The roof of each house rests on slender columns running close to one another, like the framework of a lattice, and, through these spaces, the owner, stretched on a long seat, can gaze out upon his grounds and watch his servants thrashing corn or gathering in the vintage, and the cattle trampling on the straw. His children play along the grass; his wife bends forward to kiss him."

Through the deepening shadows of the night pointed snouts reveal themselves here and there with ears erect and glittering eyes. Antony advances towards them. Scattering the wind in their wild rush, the animals take flight. It was a troop of jackals.

One of them remains behind, and, resting on two paws, with his body bent and his head on one side, he places himself in an attitude of defiance.

"How pretty he looks! I should like to pass my hand softly over his back."

Antony whistles to make him come near. The jackal disappears.

"Ah! he is gone to join his fellows. Oh! this solitude! this weariness!"

Laughing bitterly:

"This is such a delightful life—to twist palm branches in the fire to make shepherds' crooks, to turn out baskets and fasten mats together, and then to exchange all this handiwork with the Nomads for bread that breaks your teeth! Ah! wretched me! will there never be an end of this? But, indeed, death would be better! I can bear it no longer! Enough! Enough!"

He stamps his foot, and makes his way through the rocks with rapid step, then stops, out of breath, bursts into sobs, and flings himself upon the ground.

The night is calm; millions of stars are trembling in the sky. No sound is heard save the chattering of the tarantula.

The two arms of the cross cast a shadow on the sand. Antony, who is weeping, perceives it.

"Am I so weak, my God? Courage! Let us arise!"

He enters his cell, finds there the embers of a fire, lights a torch, and places it on the wooden stand, so as to illumine the big book.

"Suppose I take—the 'Acts of the Apostles'—yes, no matter where!

"'He saw the sky opened with a great linen sheet which was let down by its four corners, wherein were all kinds of terrestrial animals and wild beasts, reptiles and birds. And a voice said to him: Arise, Peter! Kill and eat!'

"So, then, the Lord wished that His apostle should eat every kind of food? ... whilst I ..."

Antony lets his chin sink on his breast. The rustling of the pages, which the wind scatters, causes him to lift his head, and he reads:

"'The Jews slew all their enemies with swords, and made a great carnage of them, so that they disposed at will of those whom they hated.'

"There follows the enumeration of the people slain by them—seventy-five thousand. They had endured so much! Besides, their enemies were the enemies of the true God. And how they must have enjoyed their vengeance, completely slaughtering the idolaters! No doubt the city was gorged with the dead! They must have been at the garden gates, on the staircases, and packed so closely together in the various rooms that the doors could not be closed! But here am I plunging into thoughts of murder and bloodshed!"

He opens the book at another passage.

"'Nebuchadnezzar prostrated himself with his face on the ground and adored Daniel.'

"Ah! that is good! The Most High exalts His prophets above kings. This monarch spent his life in feasting, always intoxicated with sensuality and pride. But God, to punish him, changed him into a beast, and he walked on four paws!"

Antony begins to laugh; and, while stretching out his arms, disarranges the leaves of the book with the tips of his fingers. Then his eyes fall on these words:

"'Ezechias felt great joy in coming to them. He showed them his perfumes, his gold and silver, all his aromatics, his sweet-smelling oils, all his precious vases, and the things that were in his treasures.'

"I can imagine how they beheld, heaped up to the very ceiling, gems, diamonds, darics. A man who possesses such an accumulation of these things is not the same as others. While handling them, he assumes that he holds the result of innumerable exertions, and that he has absorbed, and can again diffuse, the very life of the people. This is a useful precaution for kings. The wisest of them all was not wanting in it. His fleets brought him ivory—and apes. Where is this? It is——"

He rapidly turns over the leaves.

"Ah! this is the place:

"'The Queen of Sheba, being aware of the glory of Solomon, came to tempt him, propounding enigmas.'

"How did she hope to tempt him? The Devil was very desirous to tempt Jesus. But Jesus triumphed because He was God, and Solomon owing, perhaps, to his magical science. It is sublime, this science; for—as a philosopher has explained to me—the world forms a whole, all whose parts have an influence on one another, like the different organs of a single body. It is interesting to understand the affinities and antipathies implanted in everything by Nature, and then to put them into play. In this way one might be able to modify laws that appear to be unchangeable."

At this point the two shadows traced behind him by the arms of the cross project themselves in front of him. They form, as it were, two great horns. Antony exclaims:

"Help, my God!"

The shadows resume their former position.

"Ah! it was an illusion—nothing more. It is useless for me to torment my soul, I have no need to do so—absolutely no need!"

He sits down and crosses his arms.

"And yet methought I felt the approach ... But why should he come? Besides, do I not know his artifices? I have repelled the monstrous anchorite who, with a laugh, offered me little hot loaves; the centaur who tried to take me on his back; and that vision of a beautiful dusky maid amid the sands, which revealed itself to me as the spirit of voluptuousness."

Antony walks up and down rapidly.

"It is by my direction that all these holy retreats have been built, full of monks wearing hair-cloths beneath their goatskins, and numerous enough to furnish forth an army. I have healed diseases at a distance. I have banished demons. I have waded through the river in the midst of crocodiles. The Emperor Constantine has written me three letters; and Balacius, who treated with contempt the letter I sent him, has been torn by his own horses. The people of Alexandria, whenever I reappeared amongst them, fought to get a glimpse of me; and Athanasius was my guide when I took my departure. But what toils, too, I have had to undergo! Here, for more than thirty years, have I been constantly groaning in the desert! I have carried on my loins eighty pounds of bronze, like Eusebius; I have exposed my body to the stings of insects, like Macarius; I have remained fifty-three nights without closing an eye, like Pachomius; and those who are decapitated, torn with pincers, or burnt, possess less virtue, perhaps, inasmuch as my life is a continual martyrdom!"

Antony slackens his pace.

"Certainly there is no one who undergoes so much mortification. Charitable hearts are growing fewer, and people never give me anything now. My cloak is worn out, and I have no sandals, nor even a porringer; for I gave all my goods and chattels to the poor and my own family, without keeping a single obolus for myself. Should I not need a little money to get the tools that are indispensable for my work? Oh! not much—a little sum! ... I would husband it.

"The Fathers of Nicæa were ranged in purple robes on thrones along the wall, like the Magi; and they were entertained at a banquet, while honours were heaped upon them, especially on Paphnutius, merely because he has lost an eye and is lame since Dioclesian's persecution! Many a time the Emperor has kissed his injured eye. What folly! Moreover, the Council had such worthless members! Theophilus, a bishop of Scythia; John, another, in Persia; Spiridion, a cattle-drover. Alexander was too old. Athanasius ought to have made himself more agreeable to the Arians in order to get concessions from them!

"How is it they dealt with me? They would not even give me a hearing! He who spoke against me—a tall young man with a curling beard—coolly launched out captious objections; and while I was trying to find words to reply to him, they kept looking at me with malignant glances, barking at me like hyenas. Ah! if I could only get them all sent into exile by the Emperor, or rather smite them, crush them, behold them suffering. I have much to suffer myself!"

He sinks swooning against the wall of his cell.

"This is what it is to have fasted overmuch! My strength is going. If I had eaten, only once, a morsel of meat!"

He half-closes his eyes languidly.

"Ah! for some red flesh ... a bunch of grapes to nibble, some curds that would quiver on a plate!

"But what ails me now? What ails me now? I feel my heart dilating like the sea when it swells before the storm. An overwhelming weakness bows me down, and the warm atmosphere seems to waft towards me the odour of hair. Still, there is no trace of a woman here."

He turns towards the little pathway amid the rocks.

"This is the way they come, poised in their litters on the black arms of eunuchs. They descend, and, joining together their hands, laden with rings, they kneel down. They tell me their troubles. The need of a superhuman voluptuousness tortures them. They would like to die; in their dreams they have seen gods who called them by name; and the edges of their robes fall round my feet. I repel them. 'Oh! no,' they say to me, 'not yet! What must I do?' Any penance will appear easy to them. They ask me for the most severe: to share in my own, to live with me.

"It is a long time now since I have seen any of them! Perhaps, though, this is what is about to happen? And why not? If suddenly I were to hear the mule-bells ringing in the mountains. It seems to me ..."

Antony climbs upon a rock, at the entrance of the path, and bends forward, darting his eyes into the darkness.

"Yes! down there, at the very end, there is a moving mass, like people who are trying to pick their way. Here it is! They are making a mistake."

Calling out:

"On this side! Come! Come!"

The echo repeats:

"Come! Come!"

11

He lets his arms fall down, quite dazed.

"What a shame! Ah! poor Antony!"

And immediately he hears a whisper:

"Poor Antony."

"Is that anyone? Answer!"

It is the wind passing through the spaces between the rocks that causes these intonations, and in their confused sonorities he distinguishes voices, as if the air were speaking. They are low and insinuating, a kind of sibilant utterance:

The first—"Do you wish for women?"

The second—"Nay; rather great piles of money."

The third—"A shining sword."

The others—"All the people admire you."

"Go to sleep."

"You will cut their throats. Yes! you will cut their throats."

At the same time, visible objects undergo a transformation. On the edge of the cliff, the old palm-tree, with its cluster of yellow leaves, becomes the torso of a woman leaning over the abyss, and poised by her mass of hair.

Antony re-enters his cell, and the stool which sustains the big book, with its pages filled with black letters, seems to him a bush covered with swallows.

"Without doubt, it is the torch that is making this play of light. Let us put it out!"

He puts it out, and finds himself in profound darkness.

And, suddenly, through the midst of the air, passes first, a pool of water, then a prostitute, the corner of a temple, a figure of a soldier, and a chariot with two white horses prancing.

These images make their appearance abruptly, in successive shocks, standing out from the darkness like pictures of scarlet above a background of ebony.

Their motion becomes more rapid; they pass in a dizzy fashion. At other times they stop, and, growing pale by degrees, dissolve—or, rather, they fly away, and instantly others arrive in their stead.

Antony droops his eyelids.

They multiply, surround, besiege him. An unspeakable terror seizes hold of him, and he no longer has any sensation but that of a burning contraction in the epigastrium. In spite of the confusion of his brain, he is conscious of a tremendous silence which separates him from all the world. He tries to speak; impossible! It is as if the link that bound him to existence was snapped; and, making no further resistance, Antony falls upon the mat.

CHAPTER II

The Temptation of Love and Power

THEN, a great shadow—more subtle than an ordinary shadow, from whose borders other shadows hang in festoons—traces itself upon the ground.

It is the Devil, resting against the roof of the cell and carrying under his wings—like a gigantic bat that is suckling its young—the Seven Deadly Sins, whose grinning heads disclose themselves confusedly.

Antony, his eyes still closed, remains languidly passive, and stretches his limbs upon the mat, which seems to him to grow softer every moment, until it swells out and becomes a bed; then the bed becomes a shallop, with water rippling against its sides.

To right and left rise up two necks of black soil that tower above the cultivated plains, with a sycamore here and there. A noise of bells, drums, and singers resounds at a distance. These are caused by people who are going down from Canopus to sleep at the Temple of Serapis. Antony is aware of this, and he glides, driven by the wind, between the two banks of the canal. The leaves of the papyrus and the red blossoms of the water-lilies, larger than a man, bend over him. He lies extended at the bottom of the vessel. An oar from behind drags through the water. From time to time rises a hot breath of air that shakes the thin reeds. The murmur of the tiny waves grows fainter. A drowsiness takes possession of him. He dreams that he is an Egyptian Solitary.

Then he starts up all of a sudden.

"Have I been dreaming? It was so pleasant that I doubted its reality. My tongue is burning! I am thirsty!"

He enters his cell and searches about everywhere at random.

14

"The ground is wet! Has it been raining? Stop! Scraps of food! My pitcher broken! But the water-bottle?"

He finds it.

"Empty, completely empty! In order to get down to the river, I should need three hours at least, and the night is so dark I could not see well enough to find my way there. My entrails are writhing. Where is the bread?"

After searching for some time he picks up a crust smaller than an egg.

"How is this? The jackals must have taken it, curse them!"

And he flings the bread furiously upon the ground.

This movement is scarcely completed when a table presents itself to view, covered with all kinds of dainties. The table-cloth of byssus, striated like the fillets of sphinxes, seems to unfold itself in luminous undulations. Upon it there are enormous quarters of flesh-meat, huge fishes, birds with their feathers, quadrupeds with their hair, fruits with an almost natural colouring; and pieces of white ice and flagons of violet crystal shed glowing reflections. In the middle of the table Antony observes a wild boar smoking from all its pores, its paws beneath its belly, its eyes half-closed — and the idea of being able to eat this formidable animal rejoices his heart exceedingly. Then, there are things he had never seen before — black hashes, jellies of the colour of gold, ragoûts, in which mushrooms float like water-lilies on the surface of a pool, whipped creams, so light that they resemble clouds.

And the aroma of all this brings to him the odour of the ocean, the coolness of fountains, the mighty perfume of woods. He dilates his nostrils as much as possible; he drivels, saying to himself that there is enough there to last for a year, for ten years, for his whole life!

In proportion as he fixes his wide-opened eyes upon the dishes, others accumulate, forming a pyramid, whose angles turn

15

downwards. The wines begin to flow, the fishes to palpitate; the blood in the dishes bubbles up; the pulp of the fruits draws nearer, like amorous lips; and the table rises to his breast, to his very chin— with only one seat and one cover, which are exactly in front of him.

He is about to seize the loaf of bread. Other loaves make their appearance.

"For me! ... all! but— —"

Antony draws back.

"In the place of the one which was there, here are others! It is a miracle, then, exactly like that the Lord performed! ... With what object? Nay, all the rest of it is not less incomprehensible! Ah! demon, begone! begone!"

He gives a kick to the table. It disappears.

"Nothing more? No!"

He draws a long breath.

"Ah! the temptation was strong. But what an escape I have had!"

He raises up his head, and stumbles against an object which emits a sound.

"What can this be?"

Antony stoops down.

"Hold! A cup! Someone must have lost it while travelling—nothing extraordinary!—--"

He wets his finger and rubs.

"It glitters! Precious metal! However, I cannot distinguish— —"

He lights his torch and examines the cup.

"It is made of silver, adorned with ovolos at its rim, with a medal at the bottom."

He makes the medal resound with a touch of his finger-nail.

"It is a piece of money which is worth from seven to eight drachmas—not more. No matter! I can easily with that sum get myself a sheepskin."

The torch's reflection lights up the cup.

"It is not possible! Gold! yes, all gold!"

He finds another piece, larger than the first, at the bottom, and, underneath that many others.

"Why, here's a sum large enough to buy three cows—a little field!"

The cup is now filled with gold pieces.

"Come, then! a hundred slaves, soldiers, a heap wherewith to buy——"

Here the granulations of the cup's rim, detaching themselves, form a pearl necklace.

"With this jewel here, one might even win the Emperor's wife!"

With a shake Antony makes the necklace slip over his wrist. He holds the cup in his left hand, and with his right arm raises the torch to shed more light upon it. Like water trickling down from a basin, it pours itself out in continuous waves, so as to make a hillock on the sand—diamonds, carbuncles, and sapphires mingled with huge pieces of gold bearing the effigies of kings.

"What? What? Staters, shekels, darics, aryandics! Alexander, Demetrius, the Ptolemies, Cæsar! But each of them had not as much! Nothing impossible in it! More to come! And those rays which dazzle me! Ah! my heart overflows! How good this is! Yes! ... Yes! ... more! Never enough! It did not matter even if I kept flinging it into the sea; more would remain. Why lose any of it? I will keep it all, without telling anyone about it. I will dig myself a chamber in the rock, the interior of which will be lined with strips of bronze; and thither will I come to feel the piles of gold sinking under my heels. I will plunge my arms into it as if into sacks of corn. I would like to anoint my face with it—to sleep on top of it!"

He lets go the torch in order to embrace the heap, and falls to the ground on his breast. He gets up again. The place is perfectly empty!

"What have I done? If I died during that brief space of time, the result would have been Hell—irrevocable Hell!"

A shudder runs through his frame.

"So, then, I am accursed? Ah! no, this is all my own fault! I let myself be caught in every trap. There is no one more idiotic or more infamous. I would like to beat myself, or, rather, to tear myself out of my body. I have restrained myself too long. I need to avenge myself, to strike, to kill! It is as if I had a troop of wild beasts in my soul. I would like, with a stroke of a hatchet in the midst of a crowd——Ah! a dagger! ..."

He flings himself upon his knife, which he has just seen. The knife slips from his hand, and Antony remains propped against the wall of his cell, his mouth wide open, motionless—like one in a trance.

All the surroundings have disappeared.

He finds himself in Alexandria on the Panium—an artificial mound raised in the centre of the city, with corkscrew stairs on the outside.

In front of it stretches Lake Mareotis, with the sea to the right and the open plain to the left, and, directly under his eyes, an irregular succession of flat roofs, traversed from north to south and from east to west by two streets, which cross each other, and which form, in their entire length, a row of porticoes with Corinthian capitals. The houses overhanging this double colonnade have stained-glass windows. Some have enormous wooden cages outside of them, in which the air from without is swallowed up.

Monuments in various styles of architecture are piled close to one another. Egyptian pylons rise above Greek temples. Obelisks exhibit themselves like spears between battlements of red brick. In the centres of squares there are statues of Hermes with pointed ears, and of Anubis with dogs' heads. Antony notices the mosaics in the court-yards, and the tapestries hung from the cross-beams of the ceiling.

With a single glance he takes in the two ports (the Grand Port and the Eunostus), both round like two circles, and separated by a mole joining Alexandria to the rocky island, on which stands the tower of the Pharos, quadrangular, five hundred cubits high and in nine storys, with a heap of black charcoal flaming on its summit.

Small ports nearer to the shore intersect the principal ports. The mole is terminated at each end by a bridge built on marble columns fixed in the sea. Vessels pass beneath, and pleasure-boats inlaid with ivory, gondolas covered with awnings, triremes and biremes, all kinds of shipping, move up and down or remain at anchor along the quays.

Around the Grand Port there is an uninterrupted succession of Royal structures: the palace of the Ptolemies, the Museum, the Posideion, the Cæsarium, the Timonium where Mark Antony took refuge, and the Soma which contains the tomb of Alexander; while at the other extremity of the city, close to the Eunostus, might be seen glass, perfume, and paper factories.

Itinerant vendors, porters, and ass-drivers rush to and fro, jostling against one another. Here and there a priest of Osiris with a panther's skin on his shoulders, a Roman soldier, or a group of negroes, may be observed. Women stop in front of stalls where artisans are at work, and the grinding of chariot-wheels frightens away some birds who are picking up from the ground the sweepings of the shambles and the remnants of fish. Over the uniformity of white houses the plan of the streets casts, as it were, a black network. The markets, filled with herbage, exhibit green bouquets, the drying-sheds of the dyers, plates of colours, and the gold ornaments on the pediments of temples, luminous points—all this contained within the oval enclosure of the greyish walls, under the vault of the blue heavens, hard by the motionless sea. But the crowd stops and looks towards the eastern side, from which enormous whirlwinds of dust are advancing.

It is the monks of the Thebaïd who are coming, clad in goats' skins, armed with clubs, and howling forth a canticle of war and of religion with this refrain:

"Where are they? Where are they?"

Antony comprehends that they have come to kill the Arians.

All at once, the streets are deserted, and one sees no longer anything but running feet.

And now the Solitaries are in the city. Their formidable cudgels, studded with nails, whirl around like monstrances of steel. One can hear the crash of things being broken in the houses. Intervals of silence follow, and then the loud cries burst forth again. From one end of the streets to the other there is a continuous eddying of people in a state of terror. Several are armed with pikes. Sometimes two groups meet and form into one; and this multitude, after rushing along the pavements, separates, and those composing it proceed to knock one another down. But the men with long hair always reappear.

Thin wreaths of smoke escape from the corners of buildings. The leaves of the doors burst asunder; the skirts of the walls fall in; the architraves topple over.

Antony meets all his enemies one after another. He recognises people whom he had forgotten. Before killing them, he outrages them. He rips them open, cuts their throats, knocks them down,

20

drags the old men by their beards, runs over children, and beats those who are wounded. People revenge themselves on luxury. Those who cannot read, tear the books to pieces; others smash and destroy the statues, the paintings, the furniture, the cabinets—a thousand dainty objects whose use they are ignorant of, and which, for that very reason, exasperate them. From time to time they stop, out of breath, and then begin again. The inhabitants, taking refuge in the court-yards, utter lamentations. The women lift their eyes to Heaven, weeping, with their arms bare. In order to move the Solitaries they embrace their knees; but the latter only dash them aside, and the blood gushes up to the ceiling, falls back on the linen clothes that line the walls, streams from the trunks of decapitated corpses, fills the aqueducts, and rolls in great red pools along the ground.

Antony is steeped in it up to his middle. He steps into it, sucks it up with his lips, and quivers with joy at feeling it on his limbs and under his hair, which is quite wet with it.

The night falls. The terrible clamour abates.

The Solitaries have disappeared.

Suddenly, on the outer galleries lining the nine stages of the Pharos, Antony perceives thick black lines, as if a flock of crows had alighted there. He hastens thither, and soon finds himself on the summit.

A huge copper mirror turned towards the sea reflects the ships in the offing.

Antony amuses himself by looking at them; and as he continues looking at them, their number increases.

They are gathered in a gulf formed like a crescent. Behind, upon a promontory, stretches a new city built in the Roman style of architecture, with cupolas of stone, conical roofs, marble work in red and blue, and a profusion of bronze attached to the volutes of capitals, to the tops of houses, and to the angles of cornices. A wood, formed of cypress-trees, overhangs it. The colour of the sea is greener; the air is colder. On the mountains at the horizon there is snow.

Antony is about to pursue his way when a man accosts him, and says:

"Come! they are waiting for you!"

He traverses a forum, enters a court-yard, stoops under a gate, and he arrives before the front of the palace, adorned with a group in wax representing the Emperor Constantine hurling the dragon to the earth. A porphyry basin supports in its centre a golden conch filled with pistachio-nuts. His guide informs him that he may take some of them. He does so.

Then he loses himself, as it were, in a succession of apartments.

Along the walls may be seen, in mosaic, generals offering conquered cities to the Emperor on the palms of their hands. And on every side are columns of basalt, gratings of silver filigree, seats of ivory, and tapestries embroidered with pearls. The light falls from the vaulted roof, and Antony proceeds on his way. Tepid exhalations spread around; occasionally he hears the modest patter of a sandal. Posted in the ante-chambers, the custodians—who resemble automatons—bear on their shoulders vermilion-coloured truncheons.

At last, he finds himself in the lower part of a hall with hyacinth curtains at its extreme end. They divide, and reveal the Emperor seated upon a throne, attired in a violet tunic and red buskins with black bands.

A diadem of pearls is wreathed around his hair, which is arranged in symmetrical rolls. He has drooping eyelids, a straight nose, and a heavy and cunning expression of countenance. At the corners of the daïs, extended above his head, are placed four golden doves, and, at the foot of the throne, two enamelled lions are squatted. The doves begin to coo, the lions to roar. The Emperor rolls his eyes; Antony steps forward; and directly, without preamble, they proceed with a narrative of events.

"In the cities of Antioch, Ephesus, and Alexandria, the temples have been pillaged, and the statues of the gods converted into pots and porridge-pans."

The Emperor laughs heartily at this. Antony reproaches him for his tolerance towards the Novatians. But the Emperor flies into a passion. "Novatians, Arians, Meletians—he is sick of them all!" However, he admires the episcopacy, for the Christians create bishops, who depend on five or six personages, and it is his interest to gain over the latter in order to have the rest on his side. Moreover, he has not failed to furnish them with considerable sums. But he detests the fathers of the Council of Nicæa. "Come, let us have a look at them."

Antony follows him. And they are found on the same floor under a terrace which commands a view of a hippodrome full of people, and surmounted by porticoes wherein the rest of the crowd are walking to and fro. In the centre of the course there is a narrow platform on which stands a miniature temple of Mercury, a statue of Constantine, and three bronze serpents intertwined with each other; while at one end there are three huge wooden eggs, and at the other seven dolphins with their tails in the air.

Behind the Imperial pavilion, the prefects of the chambers, the lords of the household, and the Patricians are placed at intervals as far as the first story of a church, all whose windows are lined with women. At the right is the gallery of the Blue faction, at the left that of the Green, while below there is a picket of soldiers, and, on a level with the arena, a row of Corinthian pillars, forming the entrance to the stalls.

The races are about to begin; the horses fall into line. Tall plumes fixed between their ears sway in the wind like trees; and in their leaps they shake the chariots in the form of shells, driven by coachmen wearing a kind of many-coloured cuirass with sleeves narrow at the wrists and wide in the arms, with legs uncovered, full beard, and hair shaven above the forehead after the fashion of the Huns.

Antony is deafened by the murmuring of voices. Above and below he perceives nothing but painted faces, motley garments, and plates of worked gold; and the sand of the arena, perfectly white, shines like a mirror.

The Emperor converses with him, confides to him some important secrets, informs him of the assassination of his own son Crispus, and goes so far as to consult Antony about his health.

Meanwhile, Antony perceives slaves at the end of the stalls. They are the fathers of the Council of Nicæa, in rags, abject. The martyr Paphnutius is brushing a horse's mane; Theophilus is scrubbing the legs of another; John is painting the hoofs of a third; while Alexander is picking up their droppings in a basket.

Antony passes among them. They salaam to him, beg of him to intercede for them, and kiss his hands. The entire crowd hoots at them; and he rejoices in their degradation immeasurably. And now he has become one of the great ones of the Court, the Emperor's confidant, first minister! Constantine places the diadem on his forehead, and Antony keeps it, as if this honour were quite natural to him.

And presently is disclosed, beneath the darkness, an immense hall, lighted up by candelabra of gold.

Columns, half lost in shadow so tall are they, run in a row behind the tables, which stretch to the horizon, where appear, in a luminous haze, staircases placed one above another, successions of archways, colossi, towers; and, in the background, an unoccupied wing of the palace, which cedars overtop, making blacker masses above the darkness.

The guests, crowned with violets, lean upon their elbows on low-lying couches. Beside each one are placed amphorae, from which they pour out wine; and, at the very end, by himself, adorned with the tiara and covered with carbuncles, King Nebuchadnezzar is eating and drinking. To right and left of him, two theories of priests, with peaked caps, are swinging censers. Upon the ground are crawling captive kings, without feet or hands, to whom he flings bones to pick. Further down stand his brothers, with shades over their eyes, for they are perfectly blind.

A constant lamentation ascends from the depths of the ergastula. The soft and monotonous sounds of a hydraulic organ alternate with the chorus of voices; and one feels as if all around the hall there was an immense city, an ocean of humanity, whose waves were beating against the walls.

The slaves rush forward carrying plates. Women run about offering drink to the guests. The baskets groan under the load of bread, and a dromedary, laden with leathern bottles, passes to and fro, letting vervain trickle over the floor in order to cool it.

Belluarii lead forth lions; dancing-girls, with their hair in ringlets, turn somersaults, while squirting fire through their nostrils; negro-jugglers perform tricks; naked children fling snowballs, which, in falling, crash against the shining silver plate. The clamour is so dreadful that it might be described as a tempest, and the steam of the viands, as well as the respirations of the guests, spreads, as it were, a cloud over the feast. Now and then, flakes from the huge torches, snatched away by the wind, traverse the night like flying stars.

The King wipes off the perfumes from his visage with his hand. He eats from the sacred vessels, and then breaks them, and he enumerates, mentally, his fleets, his armies, his peoples. Presently, through a whim, he will burn his palace, along with his guests. He calculates on rebuilding the Tower of Babel, and dethroning God.

Antony reads, at a distance, on his forehead, all his thoughts. They take possession of himself—and he becomes Nebuchadnezzar.

25

Immediately, he is satiated with conquests and exterminations; and a longing seizes him to plunge into every kind of vileness. Moreover, the degradation wherewith men are terrified is an outrage done to their souls, a means still more of stupefying them; and, as nothing is lower than a brute beast, Antony falls upon four paws on the table, and bellows like a bull.

He feels a pain in his hand—a pebble, as it happened, has hurt him—and he again finds himself in his cell.

The rocky enclosure is empty. The stars are shining. All is silence.

"Once more I have been deceived. Why these things? They arise from the revolts of the flesh! Ah! miserable man that I am!"

He dashes into his cell, takes out of it a bundle of cords, with iron nails at the ends of them, strips himself to the waist, and raising his eyes towards Heaven:

"Accept my penance, O my God! Do not despise it on account of its insufficiency. Make it sharp, prolonged, excessive. It is time! To work!"

He proceeds to lash himself vigorously.

"Ah! no! no! No pity!"

He begins again.

"Oh! Oh! Oh! Each stroke tears my skin, cuts my limbs. This smarts horribly! Ah! it is not so terrible! One gets used to it. It seems to me even ..."

Antony stops.

"Come on, then, coward! Come on, then! Good! good! On the arms, on the back, on the breast, against the belly, everywhere! Hiss, thongs! bite me! tear me! I would like the drops of my blood to gush forth to the stars, to break my back, to strip my nerves bare!

Pincers! wooden horses! molten lead! The martyrs bore more than that! Is that not so, Ammonaria?"

The shadows of the Devil's horns reappear.

"I might have been fastened to the pillar next to yours, face to face with you, under your very eyes, responding to your shrieks with my sighs, and our griefs would blend into one, and our souls would commingle."

He flogs himself furiously.

"Hold! hold! for your sake! once more! ... But this is a mere tickling that passes through my frame. What torture! What delight! Those are like kisses. My marrow is melting! I am dying!"

And in front of him he sees three cavaliers, mounted on wild asses, clad in green garments, holding lilies in their hands, and all resembling one another in figure.

Antony turns back, and sees three other cavaliers of the same kind, mounted on similar wild asses, in the same attitude.

He draws back. Then the wild asses, all at the same time, step forward a pace or two, and rub their snouts against him, trying to bite his garment. Voices exclaim, "This way! this way! Here is the place!" And banners appear between the clefts of the mountain, with camels' heads in halters of red silk, mules laden with baggage, and women covered with yellow veils, mounted astride on piebald horses.

The panting animals lie down; the slaves fling themselves on the bales of goods, roll out the variegated carpets, and strew the ground with glittering objects.

A white elephant, caparisoned with a fillet of gold, runs along, shaking the bouquet of ostrich feathers attached to his head-band.

On his back, lying on cushions of blue wool, cross-legged, with eyelids half-closed and well-poised head, is a woman so magnificently attired that she emits rays around her. The attendants prostrate themselves, the elephant bends his knees, and the Queen of Sheba, gliding down by his shoulder, steps lightly on the carpet and advances towards Antony. Her robe of gold brocade, regularly divided by furbelows of pearls, jet and sapphires, is drawn tightly round her waist by a close-fitting corsage, set off with a variety of colours representing the twelve signs of the Zodiac. She wears high-heeled pattens, one of which is black and strewn with silver stars and a crescent, whilst the other is white and is covered with drops of gold, with a sun in their midst.

Her loose sleeves, garnished with emeralds and birds' plumes, exposes to view her little, rounded arms, adorned at the wrists with bracelets of ebony; and her hands, covered with rings, are terminated by nails so pointed that the ends of her fingers are almost like needles.

A chain of plate gold, passing under her chin, runs along her cheeks till it twists itself in spiral fashion around her head, over which blue powder is scattered; then, descending, it slips over her shoulders and is fastened above her bosom by a diamond scorpion, which stretches out its tongue between her breasts. From her ears hang two great white pearls. The edges of her eyelids are painted black. On her left cheek-bone she has a natural brown spot, and when she opens her mouth she breathes with difficulty, as if her bodice distressed her.

As she comes forward, she swings a green parasol with an ivory handle surrounded by vermilion bells; and twelve curly negro boys carry the long train of her robe, the end of which is held by an ape, who raises it every now and then.

She says:

"Ah! handsome hermit! handsome hermit! My heart is faint! By dint of stamping with impatience my heels have grown hard, and I have split one of my toe-nails. I sent out shepherds, who posted themselves on the mountains, with their bands stretched over their eyes, and searchers, who cried out your name in the woods, and scouts, who ran along the different roads, saying to each passer-by: 'Have you seen him?'

"At night I shed tears with my face turned to the wall. My tears, in the long run, made two little holes in the mosaic-work—like pools of water in rocks—for I love you! Oh! yes; very much!"

She catches his beard.

"Smile on me, then, handsome hermit! Smile on me, then! You will find I am very gay! I play on the lyre, I dance like a bee, and I can tell many stories, each one more diverting than the last.

"You cannot imagine what a long journey we have made. Look at the wild asses of the green-clad couriers—dead through fatigue!"

The wild asses are stretched motionless on the ground.

"For three great moons they have journeyed at an even pace, with pebbles in their teeth to cut the wind, their tails always erect, their hams always bent, and always in full gallop. You will not find their equals. They came to me from my maternal grandfather, the Emperor Saharil, son of Jakhschab, son of Jaarab, son of Kastan. Ah! if they were still living, we would put them under a litter in order to get home quickly. But ... how now? ... What are you thinking of?"

She inspects him.

"Ah! when you are my husband, I will clothe you, I will fling perfumes over you, I will pick out your hairs."

Antony remains motionless, stiffer than a stake, pale as a corpse.

"You have a melancholy air: is it at quitting your cell? Why, I have given up everything for your sake—even King Solomon, who has, no doubt, much wisdom, twenty thousand war-chariots, and a lovely beard! I have brought you my wedding presents. Choose."

She walks up and down between the row of slaves and the merchandise.

"Here is balsam of Genesareth, incense from Cape Gardefan, ladanum, cinnamon and silphium, a good thing to put into sauces. There are within Assyrian embroideries, ivories from the Ganges, and the purple cloth of Elissa; and this case of snow contains a bottle of Chalybon, a wine reserved for the Kings of Assyria, which is drunk pure out of the horn of a unicorn. Here are collars, clasps, fillets, parasols, gold dust from Baasa, tin from Tartessus, blue wood from Pandion, white furs from Issidonia, carbuncles from the island of Palæsimundum, and tooth-picks made with the hair of the tachas—an extinct animal found under the earth. These cushions are from Emathia, and these mantle-fringes from Palmyra. Under this Babylonian carpet there are ... but come, then! Come, then!"

She pulls Saint Antony along by the beard. He resists. She goes on:

"This light tissue, which crackles under the fingers with the noise of sparks, is the famous yellow linen brought by the merchants from Bactriana. They required no less than forty-three interpreters during their voyage. I will make garments of it for you, which you will put on at home.

"Press the fastenings of that sycamore box, and give me the ivory casket in my elephant's packing-case!"

They draw out of a box some round objects covered with a veil, and bring her a little case covered with carvings.

"Would you like the buckler of Dgian-ben-Dgian, the builder of the Pyramids? Here it is! It is composed of seven dragons' skins placed one above another, joined by diamond screws, and tanned in the bile of a parricide. It represents, on one side, all the wars which have taken place since the invention of arms, and, on the other, all the wars that will take place till the end of the world. Above, the thunderbolt rebounds like a ball of cork. I am going to put it on your arm, and you will carry it to the chase.

30

"But if you knew what I have in my little case! Try to open it! Nobody has succeeded in doing that. Embrace me, and I will tell you."

She takes Saint Antony by the two cheeks. He repels her with outstretched arms.

"It was one night when King Solomon had lost his head. At length, we had concluded a bargain. He arose, and, going out with the stride of a wolf ..."

She dances a pirouette.

"Ah! ah! handsome hermit! you shall not know it! you shall not know it!"

She shakes her parasol, and all the little bells begin to ring.

"I have many other things besides—there, now! I have treasures shut up in galleries, where they are lost as in a wood. I have summer palaces of lattice-reeds, and winter palaces of black marble. In the midst of great lakes, like seas, I have islands round as pieces of silver all covered with mother-of-pearl, whose shores make music with the beating of the liquid waves that roll over the sand. The slaves of my kitchen catch birds in my aviaries, and angle for fish in my ponds. I have engravers continually sitting to stamp my likeness on hard stones, panting workers in bronze who cast my statues, and perfumers who mix the juice of plants with vinegar and beat up pastes. I have dressmakers who cut out stuffs for me, goldsmiths who make jewels for me, women whose duty it is to select head-dresses for me, and attentive house-painters pouring over my panellings boiling resin, which they cool with fans. I have attendants for my harem, eunuchs enough to make an army. And then I have armies, subjects! I have in my vestibule a guard of dwarfs, carrying on their backs ivory trumpets."

Antony sighs.

"I have teams of gazelles, quadrigæ of elephants, hundreds of

31

camels, and mares with such long manes that their feet get entangled with them when they are galloping, and flocks with such huge horns that the woods are torn down in front of them when they are pasturing. I have giraffes who walk in my gardens, and who raise their heads over the edge of my roof when I am taking the air after dinner. Seated in a shell, and drawn by dolphins, I go up and down the grottoes, listening to the water flowing from the stalactites. I journey to the diamond country, where my friends the magicians allow me to choose the most beautiful; then I ascend to earth once more, and return home."

She gives a piercing whistle, and a large bird, descending from the sky, alights on the top of her head-dress, from which he scatters the blue powder. His plumage, of orange colour, seems composed of metallic scales. His dainty head, adorned with a silver tuft, exhibits a human visage. He has four wings, a vulture's claws, and an immense peacock's tail, which he displays in a ring behind him. He seizes in his beak the Queen's parasol, staggers a little before he finds his equilibrium, then erects all his feathers, and remains motionless.

"Thanks, fair Simorg-anka! You who have brought me to the place where the lover is concealed! Thanks! thanks! messenger of my heart! He flies like desire. He travels all over the world. In the evening he returns; he lies down at the foot of my couch; he tells me what he has seen, the seas he has flown over, with their fishes and their ships, the great empty deserts which he has looked down upon from his airy height in the skies, all the harvests bending in the fields, and the plants that shoot up on the walls of abandoned cities."

She twists her arms with a languishing air.

"Oh! if you were willing! if you were only willing! ... I have a pavilion on a promontory, in the midst of an isthmus between two oceans. It is wainscotted with plates of glass, floored with tortoise-shells, and is open to the four winds of Heaven. From above, I watch the return of my fleets and the people who ascend the hill with loads on their shoulders. We should sleep on down softer than clouds; we should drink cool draughts out of the rinds of fruit, and we gaze at the sun through a canopy of emeralds. Come!"

Antony recoils. She draws close to him, and, in a tone of irritation:

"How so? Rich, coquettish, and in love?—is not that enough for you, eh? But must she be lascivious, gross, with a hoarse voice, a head of hair like fire, and rebounding flesh? Do you prefer a body cold as a serpent's skin, or, perchance, great black eyes more sombre than mysterious caverns? Look at these eyes of mine, then!"

Antony gazes at them, in spite of himself.

"All the women you ever have met, from the daughter of the cross-roads singing beneath her lantern to the fair patrician scattering leaves from the top of her litter, all the forms you have caught a glimpse of, all the imaginings of your desire, ask for them! I am not a woman—I am a world. My garments have but to fall, and you shall discover upon my person a succession of mysteries."

Antony's teeth chattered.

"If you placed your finger on my shoulder, it would be like a stream of fire in your veins. The possession of the least part of my body will fill you with a joy more vehement than the conquest of an empire. Bring your lips near! My kisses have the taste of fruit which would melt in your heart. Ah! how you will lose yourself in my tresses, caress my breasts, marvel at my limbs, and be scorched by my eyes, between my arms, in a whirlwind——"

Antony makes the sign of the Cross.

"So, then, you disdain me! Farewell!"

She turns away weeping; then she returns.

"Are you quite sure? So lovely a woman?"

She laughs, and the ape who holds the end of her robe lifts it up.

"You will repent, my fine hermit! you will groan; you will be sick of life! but I will mock at you! la! la! la! oh! oh! oh!"

She goes off with her hands on her waist, skipping on one foot.

The slaves file off before Saint Antony's face, together with the horses, the dromedaries, the elephant, the attendants, the mules, once more covered with their loads, the negro boys, the ape, and the green-clad couriers holding their broken lilies in their hands— and the Queen of Sheba departs, with a spasmodic utterance which might be either a sob or a chuckle.

CHAPTER III

The Disciple, Hilarion

WHEN she has disappeared, Antony perceives a child on the threshold of his cell.

"It is one of the Queen's servants," he thinks.

This child is small, like a dwarf, and yet thickset, like one of the Cabiri, distorted, and with a miserable aspect. White hair covers his prodigiously large head, and he shivers under a sorry tunic, while he grasps in his hand a roll of papyrus. The light of the moon, across which a cloud is passing, falls upon him.

Antony observes him from a distance, and is afraid of him.

"Who are you?"

The child replies:

"Your former disciple, Hilarion."

Antony—"You lie! Hilarion has been living for many years in Palestine."

Hilarion—"I have returned from it! It is I, in good sooth!"

Antony, draws closer and inspects him—"Why, his figure was bright as the dawn, open, joyous. This one is quite sombre, and has an aged look."

Hilarion—"I am worn out with constant toiling."

Antony—"The voice, too, is different. It has a tone that chills you."

Hilarion—"That is because I nourish myself on bitter fare."

Antony—"And those white locks?"

35

Hilarion—"I have had so many griefs."

Antony, aside—"Can it be possible? ..."

Hilarion—"I was not so far away as you imagined. The hermit, Paul, paid you a visit this year during the month of Schebar. It is just twenty days since the nomads brought you bread. You told a sailor the day before yesterday to send you three bodkins."

Antony—"He knows everything!"

Hilarion—"Learn, too, that I have never left you. But you spend long intervals without perceiving me."

Antony—"How is that? No doubt my head is troubled! To-night especially ..."

Hilarion—"All the deadly sins have arrived. But their miserable snares are of no avail against a saint like you!"

Antony—"Oh! no! no! Every minute I give way! Would that I were one of those whose souls are always intrepid and their minds firm—like the great Athanasius, for example!"

Hilarion—"He was unlawfully ordained by seven bishops!"

Antony—"What does it matter? If his virtue ..."

Hilarion—"Come, now! A haughty, cruel man, always mixed up in intrigues, and finally exiled for being a monopolist."

Antony—"Calumny!"

Hilarion—"You will not deny that he tried to corrupt Eustatius, the treasurer of the bounties?"

Antony—"So it is stated, and I admit it."

Hilarion—"He burned, for revenge, the house of Arsenius."

Antony—"Alas!"

Hilarion—"At the Council of Nicæa, he said, speaking of Jesus, 'The man of the Lord.'"

Antony—"Ah! that is a blasphemy!"

Hilarion—"So limited is he, too, that he acknowledges he knows nothing as to the nature of the Word."

Antony, smiling with pleasure—"In fact, he has not a very lofty intellect."

Hilarion—"If they had put you in his place, it would have been a great satisfaction for your brethren, as well as yourself. This life, apart from others, is a bad thing."

Antony—"On the contrary! Man, being a spirit, should withdraw himself from perishable things. All action degrades him. I would like not to cling to the earth—even with the soles of my feet."

Hilarion—"Hypocrite! who plunges himself into solitude to free himself the better from the outbreaks of his lusts! You deprive yourself of meat, of wine, of stoves, of slaves, and of honours; but how you let your imagination offer you banquets, perfumes, naked women, and applauding crowds! Your chastity is but a more subtle kind of corruption, and your contempt for the world is but the impotence of your hatred against it! This is the reason that persons like you are so lugubrious, or perhaps it is because they lack faith. The possession of the truth gives joy. Was Jesus sad? He used to go about surrounded by friends; He rested under the shade of the olive, entered the house of the publican, multiplied the cups, pardoned the fallen woman, healing all sorrows. As for you, you have no pity, save for your own wretchedness. You are so much swayed by a kind of remorse, and by a ferocious insanity, that you would repel the caress of a dog or the smile of a child."

Antony, bursts out sobbing—"Enough! Enough! You move my heart too much."

Hilarion—"Shake off the vermin from your rags! Get rid of your filth! Your God is not a Moloch who requires flesh as a sacrifice!"

37

Antony—"Still, suffering is blessed. The cherubim bend down to receive the blood of confessors."

Hilarion—"Then admire the Montanists! They surpass all the rest."

Antony—"But it is the truth of the doctrine that makes the martyr."

Hilarion—"How can he prove its excellence, seeing that he testifies equally on behalf of error?"

Antony—"Be silent, viper!"

Hilarion—"It is not perhaps so difficult. The exhortations of friends, the pleasure of outraging popular feeling, the oath they take, a certain giddy excitement—a thousand things, in fact, go to help them."

Antony draws away from Hilarion. Hilarion follows him—"Besides, this style of dying introduces great disorders. Dionysius, Cyprian, and Gregory avoided it. Peter of Alexandria has disapproved of it; and the Council of Elvira ..."

Antony, stops his ears—"I will listen to no more!"

Hilarion, raising his voice—"Here you are again falling into your habitual sin—laziness. Ignorance is the froth of pride. You say, 'My conviction is formed; why discuss the matter?' and you despise the doctors, the philosophers, tradition, and even the text of the law, of which you know nothing. Do you think you hold wisdom in your hand?"

Antony—"I am always hearing him! His noisy words fill my head."

Hilarion—"The endeavours to comprehend God are better than your mortifications for the purpose of moving him. We have no merit save our thirst for truth. Religion alone does not explain everything; and the solution of the problems which you have ignored might render it more unassailable and more sublime. Therefore, it is essential for each man's salvation that he should hold intercourse with his brethren—otherwise the Church, the assembly of the faithful, would be only a word—and that he should listen to every argument, and not disdain anything, or anyone. Balaam the soothsayer, Æschylus the poet, and the sybil of Cumæ, announced the Saviour. Dionysius the Alexandrian received from Heaven a command to read every book. Saint Clement enjoins us to study Greek literature. Hermas was converted by the illusion of a woman that he loved!"

Antony—"What an air of authority! It appears to me that you are growing taller ..."

In fact, Hilarion's height has progressively increased; and, in order not to see him, Antony closes his eyes.

Hilarion—"Make your mind easy, good hermit. Let us sit down here, on this big stone, as of yore, when, at the break of day, I used to salute you, addressing you as 'Bright morning star'; and you at once began to give me instruction. It is not finished yet. The moon affords us sufficient light. I am all attention."

He has drawn forth a calamus from his girdle, and, cross-legged on the ground, with his roll of papyrus in his hand, he raises his head towards Antony, who, seated beside him, keeps his forehead bent.

"Is not the word of God confirmed for us by the miracles? And yet the sorcerers of Pharaoh worked miracles. Other impostors could do the same; so here we may be deceived. What, then, is a miracle? An occurrence which seems to us outside the limits of Nature. But do we know all Nature's powers? And, from the mere fact that a thing ordinarily does not astonish us, does it follow that we comprehend it?"

Antony—"It matters little; we must believe in the Scripture."

Hilarion—"Saint Paul, Origen, and some others did not interpret it literally; but, if we explain it allegorically, it becomes the heritage of a limited number of people, and the evidence of its truth vanishes. What are we to do, then?"

Antony—"Leave it to the Church."

Hilarion—"Then the Scripture is useless?"

Antony—"Not at all. Although the Old Testament, I admit, has—well, obscurities ... But the New shines forth with a pure light."

Hilarion—"And yet the Angel of the Annunciation, in Matthew, appears to Joseph, whilst in Luke it is to Mary. The anointing of Jesus by a woman comes to pass, according to the First Gospel, at the beginning of his public life, but according to the three others, a few days before his death. The drink which they offer him on the Cross is, in Matthew, vinegar and gall, in Mark, wine and myrrh. If we follow Luke and Matthew, the Apostles ought to take neither money nor bag—in fact, not even sandals or a staff; while in Mark, on the contrary, Jesus forbids them to carry with them anything except sandals and a staff. Here is where I get lost ..."

Antony, in amazement—"In fact ... in fact ..."

Hilarion—"At the contact of the woman with the issue of blood, Jesus turned round, and said, 'Who has touched me?' So, then, He did not know who touched Him? That is opposed to the omniscience of Jesus. If the tomb was watched by guards, the women had not to worry themselves about an assistant to lift up the stone from the tomb. Therefore, there were no guards there—or rather, the holy women were not there at all. At Emmaüs, He eats with His disciples, and makes them feel His wounds. It is a human body, a material object, which can be weighed, and which, nevertheless, passes through stone walls. Is this possible?"

Antony—"It would take a good deal of time to answer you."

Hilarion—"Why did He receive the Holy Ghost, although He was the Son? What need had He of baptism, if He were the Word? How could the Devil tempt Him—God?

"Have these thoughts never occurred to you?"

40

Antony—"Yes! often! Torpid or frantic, they dwell in my conscience. I crush them out; they spring up again, they stifle me; and sometimes I believe that I am accursed."

Hilarion—"Then you have nothing to do but to serve God?"

Antony—"I have always need to adore Him."

After a prolonged silence, Hilarion resumes:

"But apart from dogma, entire liberty of research is permitted us. Do you wish to become acquainted with the hierarchy of Angels, the virtue of Numbers, the explanation of germs and metamorphoses?"

Antony—"Yes! yes! My mind is struggling to escape from its prison. It seems to me that, by gathering my forces, I shall be able to effect this. Sometimes—even for an interval brief as a lightning-flash—I feel myself, as it were, suspended in mid-air; then I fall back again!"

Hilarion—"The secret which you are anxious to possess is guarded by sages. They live in a distant country, sitting under gigantic trees, robed in white, and calm as gods. A warm atmosphere nourishes them. All around leopards stride through the plains. The murmuring of fountains mingles with the neighing of unicorns. You shall hear them; and the face of the Unknown shall be unveiled!"

Antony, sighing—"The road is long and I am old!"

Hilarion—"Oh! oh! men of learning are not rare! There are some of them even very close to you here! Let us enter!"

CHAPTER IV

The Fiery Trial

AND Antony sees in front of him an immense basilica. The light projects itself from the lower end with the magical effect of a many-coloured sun. It lights up the innumerable heads of the multitude which fills the nave and surges between the columns towards the side-aisles, where one can distinguish in the wooden compartments altars, beds, chainlets of little blue stones, and constellations painted on the walls.

In the midst of the crowd groups are stationed here and there; men standing on stools are discoursing with lifted fingers; others are praying with arms crossed, or lying down on the ground, or singing hymns, or drinking wine. Around a table the faithful are carrying on the love-feasts; martyrs are unswathing their limbs to show their wounds; old men, leaning on their staffs, are relating their travels.

Amongst them are people from the country of the Germans, from Thrace, Gaul, Scythia and the Indies—with snow on their beards, feathers in their hair, thorns in the fringes of their garments, sandals covered with dust, and skins burnt by the sun. All costumes are mingled—mantles of purple and robes of linen, embroidered dalmatics, woollen jackets, sailors' caps and bishops' mitres. Their eyes gleam strangely. They have the appearance of executioners or of eunuchs.

Hilarion advances among them. Antony, pressing against his shoulder, observes them. He notices a great many women. Several of them are dressed like men, with their hair cut short. He is afraid of them.

Hilarion—"These are the Christian women who have converted their husbands. Besides, the women are always for Jesus—even the idolaters—as witness Procula, the wife of Pilate, and Poppæa, the concubine of Nero. Don't tremble any more! Come on!"

There are fresh arrivals every moment.

They multiply; they separate, swift as shadows, all the time making a great uproar, or intermingling yells of rage, exclamations of love, canticles, and upbraidings.

Antony, in a low tone—"What do they want?"

Hilarion—"The Lord said, 'I may still have to speak to you about many things.' They possess those things."

And he pushes him towards a throne of gold, five paces off, where, surrounded by ninety-five disciples, all anointed with oil, pale and emaciated, sits the prophet Manes—beautiful as an archangel, motionless as a statue—wearing an Indian robe, with carbuncles in his plaited hair, a book of coloured pictures in his left hand, and a globe under his right. The pictures represent the creatures who are slumbering in chaos. Antony bends forward to see him. Then Manes makes his globe revolve, and, attuning his words to the music of a lyre, from which bursts forth crystalline sounds, he says:

"The celestial earth is at the upper extremity, the mortal earth at the lower. It is supported by two angels, the Splenditenens and the Omophorus, with six faces.

"At the summit of Heaven, the Impassible Divinity occupies the highest seat; underneath, face to face, are the Son of God and the Prince of Darkness.

"The darkness having made its way into His kingdom, God extracted from His essence a virtue which produced the first man; and He surrounded him with five elements. But the demons of darkness deprived him of one part, and that part is the soul.

"There is but one soul, spread through the universe, like the water of a stream divided into many channels. This it is that sighs in the

43

wind, grinds in the marble which is sawn, howls in the voice of the sea; and it sheds milky tears when the leaves are torn off the fig-tree.

"The souls that leave this world emigrate towards the stars, which are animated beings."

Antony begins to laugh:

"Ah! ah! what an absurd hallucination!"

A man, beardless, and of austere aspect—"Why?"

Antony is about to reply. But Hilarion tells him in an undertone, that this man is the mighty Origen; and Manes resumes:

"At first, they stay in the moon, where they are purified. After that, they ascend to the sun."

Antony, slowly—"I know nothing to prevent us from believing it."

Manes—"The end of every creature is the liberation of the celestial ray shut up in matter. It makes its escape more easily through perfumes, spices, the aroma of old wine, the light substances that resemble thought. But the actions of daily life withhold it. The murderer will be born again in the body of a eunuch; he who slays an animal will become that animal. If you plant a vine-tree, you will be fastened in its branches. Food absorbs those who use it. Therefore, mortify yourselves! fast!"

Hilarion—"They are temperate, as you see!"

Manes—"There is a great deal of it in flesh-meats, less in herbs. Besides, the Pure, by the force of their merits, despoil vegetables of that luminous spark, and it flies towards its source. The animals, by generation, imprison it in the flesh. Therefore, avoid women!"

Hilarion—"Admire their countenance!"

Manes—"Or, rather, act so well that they may not be prolific. It is better for the soul to sink on the earth than to languish in carnal fetters."

Antony — "Ah! abomination!"

Hilarion — "What matters the hierarchy of iniquities? The Church has done well to make marriage a sacrament!"

Saturninus, in Syrian costume — "He propagates a dismal order of things! The Father, in order to punish the rebel angels, commanded them to create the world. Christ came in order that the God of the Jews, who was one of those angels — —"

Antony — "An angel? He! the Creator?"

Gerdon — "Did He not desire to kill Moses and deceive the prophets? and did He not lead the people astray, spreading lying and idolatry?"

Marcion — "Certainly, the Creator is not the true God!"

Saint Clement of Alexandria — "Matter is eternal!"

Bardesanes, as one of the Babylonian Magi — "It was formed by the seven planetary spirits."

The Hernians — "The angels have made the souls!"

The Priscillianists — "The world was made by the Devil."

Antony, falls backward — "Horror!"

Hilarion, holding him up — "You drive yourself to despair too quickly! You don't rightly comprehend their doctrine. Here is one who has received his from Theodas, the friend of Saint Paul. Hearken to him!"

And, at a signal from Hilarion, Valentinus, in a tunic of silver cloth, with a hissing voice and a pointed skull, cries:

"The world is the work of a delirious God!"

45

Antony, hangs down his head—"The work of a delirious God!"

After a long silence:

"How is that?"

Valentinus—"The most perfect of the Æons, the Abysm, reposed on the bosom of Profundity together with Thought. From their union sprang Intelligence, who had for his consort Truth.

"Intelligence and Truth engendered the Word and Life, which in their turn engendered Man and the Church; and this makes eight Æons."

He reckons on his fingers:

"The Word and Truth produced ten other Æons, that is to say, five couples. Man and the Church produced twelve others, amongst whom were the Paraclete and Faith, Hope and Charity, Perfection and Wisdom, Sophia.

"The entire of those thirty Æons constitutes the Pleroma, or Universality of God. Thus, like the echoes of a voice that is dying away, like the exhalations of a perfume that is evaporating, like the fires of a sun that is setting, the Powers that have emanated from the Highest Powers are always growing feeble.

"But Sophia, desirous of knowing the Father, rushed out of the Pleroma; and the Word then made another pair, Christ and the Holy Ghost, who bound together all the Æons, and all together they formed Jesus, the flower of the Pleroma. Meanwhile, the effort of Sophia to escape had left in the void an image of her, an evil substance, Acharamoth. The Saviour took pity on her, and delivered her from her passions; and from the smile of Acharamoth on being set free Light was born; her tears made the waters, and her sadness engendered gloomy Matter. From Acharamoth sprang the Demiurge, the fabricator of the worlds, the heavens, and the Devil. He dwells much lower down than the Pleroma, without even beholding it, so that he imagines he is the true God, and repeats through the mouths of his prophets: 'Besides me there is no God.' Then he made man, and cast into his soul the immaterial seed, which was the Church, the reflection of the other Church placed in the Pleroma.

"Acharamoth, one day, having reached the highest region, shall unite with the Saviour; the fire hidden in the world shall annihilate all matter, shall then consume itself, and men, having become pure spirits, shall espouse the angels!"

Origen—"Then the Demon shall be conquered, and the reign of God shall begin!"

Antony represses an exclamation, and immediately Basilides, catching him by the elbow:

"The Supreme Being, with his infinite emanations, is called Abraxas, and the Saviour with all his virtues, Kaulakau, otherwise rank-upon-rank, rectitude-upon-rectitude. The power of Kaulakau is obtained by the aid of certain words inscribed on this calcedony to facilitate memory."

And he shows on his neck a little stone on which fantastic lines are engraved.

"Then you shall be transported into the invisible; and, unfettered by law, you shall despise everything, including virtue itself. As for us, the Pure, we must avoid sorrow, after the example of Kaulakau."

Antony—"What! and the Cross?"

The Elkhesaites, in hyacinthine robes, reply to him:

"The sadness, the vileness, the condemnation, and the oppression of my fathers are effaced, thanks to the new Gospel. We may deny the inferior Christ, the man-Jesus; but we must adore the other Christ generated in his person under the wing of the Dove. Honour marriage! The Holy Spirit is feminine!"

Hilarion has disappeared; and Antony, pressed forward by the crowd, finds himself facing the Carpocratians, stretched with women upon scarlet cushions:

"Before re-entering the centre of unity, you will have to pass through a series of conditions and actions. In order to free yourself from the Powers of Darkness, do their works for the present! The husband goes to his wife and says, 'Act with charity towards your brother,' and she will kiss you."

The Nicolaites, assembled around a smoking dish:

"This is meat offered to idols; let us take it! Apostacy is permitted when the heart is pure. Glut your flesh with what it asks for. Try to destroy it by means of debaucheries. Prounikos, the mother of Heaven, wallows in iniquity."

The Marcosians, with rings of gold and dripping with balsam:

"Come to us, in order to be united with the Spirit! Come to us, in order to drink immortality!"

And one of them points out to him, behind some tapestry, the body of a man with an ass's head. This represents Sabaoth, the father of the Devil. As a mark of hatred he spits upon it.

Another discloses a very low bed strewn with flowers, saying as he does so:

"The spiritual nuptials are about to be consummated."

A third holds forth a goblet of glass while he utters an invocation. Blood appears in it:

"Ah! there it is! there it is! the blood of Christ!"

Antony turns aside; but he is splashed by the water, which leaps out of a tub.

The Helvidians cast themselves into it head foremost, muttering:

"Man regenerated by baptism is incapable of sin!"

Then he passes close to a great fire, where the Adamites are warming themselves completely naked to imitate the purity of Paradise; and he jostles up against the Messalians wallowing on the stone floor half-asleep, stupid:

"Oh! run over us, if you like; we shall not budge! Work is a sin; all occupation is evil!"

Behind those, the abject Paternians, men, women, and children, pell-mell, on a heap of filth, lift up their hideous faces, besmeared with wine:

"The inferior parts of the body, having been made by the Devil, belong to him. Let us eat, drink, and enjoy!"

Ætius—"Crimes come from the need here below of the love of God!"

But all at once a man, clad in a Carthaginian mantle, jumps among them, with a bundle of thongs in his hand; and striking at random to right and left of him violently:

"Ah! imposters, brigands, simoniacs, heretics, and demons! the vermin of the schools! the dregs of Hell! This fellow here, Marcion, is a sailor from Sinope excommunicated for incest. Carpocras has been banished as a magician; Ætius has stolen his concubine; Nicolas prostituted his own wife; and Manes, who describes himself as the Buddha, and whose name is Cubricus, was flayed with the sharp end of a cane, so that his tanned skin swings at the gates of Ctesiphon."

Antony has recognised Tertullian, and rushes forward to meet him.

"Help, master! help!"

Tertullian, continuing—"Break the images! Veil the virgins! Pray, fast, weep, mortify yourselves! No philosophy! no books! After Jesus, science is useless!"

All have fled; and Antony sees, instead of Tertullian, a woman seated on a stone bench. She sobs, her head resting against a pillar, her hair hanging down, and her body wrapped in a long brown simar.

Then they find themselves close to each other far from the crowd; and a silence, an extraordinary peacefulness, ensues, such as one feels in a wood when the wind ceases and the leaves flutter no longer. This woman is very beautiful, though faded and pale as death. They stare at each other, and their eyes mutually exchange a flood of thoughts, as it were, a thousand memories of the past, bewildering and profound. At last Priscilla begins to speak:

"I was in the lowest chamber of the baths, and I was lulled to sleep by the confused murmurs that reached me from the streets. All at once I heard loud exclamations. The people cried, 'It is a magician! it is the Devil!' And the crowd stopped in front of our house opposite to the Temple of Æsculapius. I raised myself with my wrists to the height of the air-hole. On the peristyle of the temple was a man with an iron collar around his neck. He placed lighted coals on a chafing-dish, and with them made large furrows on his breast, calling out, 'Jesus! Jesus!' The people said, 'That is not lawful! let us stone him!' But he did not desist. The things that were occurring were unheard of, astounding. Flowers, large as the sun, turned around before my eyes, and I heard a harp of gold vibrating in mid-air. The day sank to its close. My arms let go the iron bars; my strength was exhausted; and when he bore me away to his house—"

Antony—"Whom are you talking about?"

Priscilla—"Why, of Montanus!"

Antony—"But Montanus is dead."

Priscilla—"That is not true."

A voice—"No, Montanus is not dead!"

Antony comes back; and near him, on the other side upon a bench,

50

a second woman is seated—this one being fair, and paler still, with swellings under her eyelids, as if she had been a long time weeping. Without waiting for him to question her, she says:

Maximilla—"We were returning from Tarsus by the mountains, when, at a turn of the road, we saw a man under a fig-tree. He cried from a distance, 'Stop!' and he sprang forward, pouring out abuse on us. The slaves rushed up to protect us. He burst out laughing. The horses pranced. The mastiffs all began to howl. He was standing up. The perspiration fell down his face. The wind made his cloak flap.

"While addressing us by name, he reproached us for the vanity of our actions, the impurity of our bodies; and he raised his fist towards the dromedaries on account of the silver bells which they wore under their jaws. His fury filled my very entrails with terror; nevertheless, it was a voluptuous sensation, which soothed, intoxicated me. At first, the slaves drew near. 'Master,' said they, 'our beasts are fatigued'; then there were the women: 'We are frightened'; and the slaves ran away. After that, the children began to cry, 'We are hungry.' And, as no answer was given to the women, they disappeared. And now he began to speak. I perceived that there was some one close beside me. It was my husband: I listened to the other. The first crawled between the stones, exclaiming, 'Do you abandon me?' and I replied, 'Yes! begone!' in order to accompany Montanus."

Antony—"A eunuch!"

Priscilla—"Ah! coarse heart, you are astonished at this! Yet Magdalen, Jane, Martha and Susanna did not enter the couch of the Saviour. Souls can be madly embraced more easily than bodies. In order to retain Eustolia with impunity, the Bishop Leontius mutilated himself—cherishing his love more than his virility. And, then, it is not my own fault. A spirit compels me to do it; Eotas cannot cure me. Nevertheless, he is cruel. What does it matter? I am the last of the prophetesses; and, after me, the end of the world will come."

51

Maximilla—"He has loaded me with his gifts. None of the others loved me so much, nor is any of them better loved."

Priscilla—"You lie! I am the person he loves!"

Maximilla—"No: it is I!"

They fight.

Between their shoulders appears a negro's head.

Montanus, covered with a black cloak, fastened by two dead men's bones:

"Be quiet, my doves! Incapable of terrestrial happiness, we by this union attain to spiritual plenitude. After the age of the Father, the age of the Son; and I inaugurate the third, that of the Paraclete. His light came to me during the forty nights when the heavenly Jerusalem shone in the firmament above my house at Pepuza.

"Ah! how you cry out with anguish when the thongs flagellate you! How your aching limbs offer themselves to my burning caresses! How you languish upon my breast with an inconceivable love! It is so strong that it has revealed new worlds to you, and you can now behold spirits with your mortal eyes."

Antony makes a gesture of astonishment.

Tertullian, coming up close to Montanus—"No doubt, since the soul has a body, that which has no body exists not."

Montanus—"In order to render it less material I have introduced numerous mortifications—three Lents every year, and, for each night, prayers, in saying which the mouth is kept closed, for fear the breath, in escaping, should sully the mental act. It is necessary to abstain from second marriages—or, rather, from marriage altogether! The angels sinned with women."

The Archontics, in hair-shirts:

"The Saviour said, 'I came to destroy the work of the woman.'"

52

The Tatianists, in hair-cloths of rushes:

"She is the tree of evil! Our bodies are the garments of skin."

And, ever advancing on the same side, Antony encounters the Valesians, stretched on the ground, with red plates below their stomachs, beneath their tunics.

They present to him a knife.

"Do like Origen and like us! Is it the pain you fear, coward? Is it the love of your flesh that restrains you, hypocrite?"

And while he watches them struggling, extended on their backs swimming in their own blood, the Cainites, with their hair fastened by vipers, pass close to him, shouting in his ears:

"Glory to Cain! Glory to Sodom! Glory to Judas!

"Cain begot the race of the strong; Sodom terrified the earth with its chastisement, and it is through Judas that God saved the world! Yes, Judas! without him no death and no Redemption!"

They pass out through the band of Circoncellions, clad in wolf-skin, crowned with thorns, and carrying iron clubs.

"Crush the fruit! Attack the fountain-head! Drown the child! Plunder the rich man who is happy, and who eats overmuch! Strike down the poor man who casts an envious glance at the ass's saddle-cloth, the dog's meal, the bird's nest, and who is grieved at not seeing others as miserable as himself.

"As for us—the Saints—in order to hasten the end of the world, we poison, burn, massacre. The only salvation is in martyrdom. We give ourselves up to martyrdom. We take off with pincers the skin of our heads; we spread our limbs under the ploughs; we cast ourselves into the mouths of furnaces. Shame on baptism! Shame on the Eucharist! Shame on marriage! Universal damnation!"

Then, throughout the basilica, there is a fresh accession of frenzy.

The Audians draw arrows against the Devil; the Collyridians fling blue veils to the ceiling; the Ascitians prostrate themselves before a wineskin; the Marcionites baptise a corpse with oil. Close beside Appelles, a woman, the better to explain her idea, shows a round loaf of bread in a bottle; another, surrounded by the Sampsians, distributes like a host the dust of her sandals. On the bed of the Marcosians, strewn with roses, two lovers embrace each other. The Circoncellions cut one another's throats; the Velesians make a rattling sound; Bardesanes sings; Carpocras dances; Maximilla and Priscilla utter loud groans; and the false prophetess of Cappadocia, quite naked, resting on a lion and brandishing three torches, yells forth the Terrible Invocation.

The pillars are poised like trunks of trees; the amulets round the necks of the Heresiarchs have lines of flame crossing each other; the constellations in the chapels move to and fro, and the walls recede under the alternate motion of the crowd, in which every head is a wave which leaps and roars.

Meanwhile, from the very depths of the uproar rises a song with bursts of laughter, in which the name of Jesus recurs. These outbursts come from the common people, who all clap their hands in order to keep time with the music. In the midst of them is Arius, in the dress of a deacon:

"The fools who declaim against me pretend to explain the absurd; and, in order to destroy them entirely, I have composed little poems so comical that they are known by heart in the mills, the taverns, and the ports.

"A thousand times no! the Son is not co-eternal with the Father, nor of the same substance. Otherwise He would not have said, 'Father, remove from Me this chalice! Why do ye call Me good? God alone is good! I go to my God, to your God!' and other expressions, proving that He was a created being. It is demonstrated to us besides by all His names: lamb, shepherd, fountain, wisdom, Son of Man, prophet, good way, corner-stone."

Sabellius—"As for me, I maintain that both are identical."

Arius—"The Council of Antioch has decided the other way."

Antony—"Who, then, is the Word? Who was Jesus?"

The Valentinians—"He was the husband of Acharamoth when she had repented!"

The Sethianians—"He was Sem, son of Noah!"

The Theodotians—"He was Melchisidech!"

The Merinthians—"He was nothing but a man!"

The Apollonarists—"He assumed the appearance of one! He simulated the Passion!"

Marcellus of Ancyra—"He is a development of the Father!"

Pope Calixtus—"Father and Son are the two forms of a single God!"

Methadius—"He was first in Adam, and then in man!"

Cerinthus—"And He will come back to life again!"

Valentinus—"Impossible—His body is celestial."

Paul of Samosta—"He is God only since His baptism."

Hermogenes—"He dwells in the sun."

And all the heresiarchs form a circle around Antony, who weeps, with his head in his hands.

A Jew, with red beard, and his skin spotted with leprosy, advances close to him, and chuckling horribly:

"His soul was the soul of Esau. He suffered from the disease of Bellerophon; and his mother, the woman who sold perfumes, surrendered herself to Pantherus, a Roman soldier, under the corn-sheaves, one harvest evening."

Antony eagerly lifts up his head, and gazes at them without uttering a word; then, treading right over them:

"Doctors, magicians, bishops and deacons, men and phantoms, back! back! Ye are all lies!"

The Heresiarchs—"We have martyrs, more martyrs than yours, prayers more difficult, higher outbursts of love, and ecstasies quite as protracted."

Antony—"But no revelation. No proofs."

Then all brandish in the air rolls of papyrus, tablets of wood, pieces of leather; and strips of cloth; and pushing them one before the other:

The Corinthians—"Here is the Gospel of the Hebrews!"

The Marcionites—"The Gospel of the Lord! The Gospel of Eve!"

The Encratites—"The Gospel of Thomas!"

The Cainites—"The Gospel of Judas!"

Basilides—"The treatise of the spirit that has come!"

Manes—"The prophecy of Barcouf!"

Antony makes a struggle and escapes them, and he perceives, in a corner filled with shadows, the old Ebionites, dried up like mummies, their glances dull, their eyebrows white.

They speak in a quavering tone:

"We have known, we ourselves have known, the carpenter's son. We were of his own age; we lived in his street. He used to amuse himself by modelling little birds with mud; without being afraid of cutting the benches, he assisted his father in his work, or rolled up, for his mother, balls of dyed wool. Then he made a journey into Egypt, whence he brought back wonderful secrets. We were in

Jericho when he discovered the eater of grasshoppers. They talked together in a low tone, without anyone being able to hear them. But it was since that occurrence that he made a noise in Galilee and that many stories have been circulated concerning him."

They repeat, tremulously:

"We have known, we ourselves; we have known him."

Antony—"One moment! Tell me! pray tell me, what was his face like?"

Tertullian—"Fierce and repulsive in its aspect; for he was laden with all the crimes, all the sorrows, and all the deformities of the world."

Antony—"Oh! no! no! I imagine, on the contrary, that there was about his entire person a superhuman beauty."

Eusebius of Cæsarea—"There is at Paneadæ, close to an old ruin, in the midst of a rank growth of weeds, a statue of stone, raised, as it is pretended, by the woman with the issue of blood. But time has gnawed away the face, and the rain has obliterated the inscription."

A woman comes forth from the group of Carpocratians.

Marcellina—"I was formerly a deaconess in a little church at Rome, where I used to show the faithful images, in silver, of St. Paul, Homer, Pythagoras and Jesus Christ.

"I have kept only his."

She draws aside the folds of her cloak.

"Do you wish it?"

A voice—"He reappears himself when we invoke him. It is the hour. Come!"

And Antony feels a brutal hand laid on him, which drags him along.

He ascends a staircase in complete darkness, and, after proceeding for some time, arrives in front of a door. Then his guide (is it Hilarion? he cannot tell) says in the ear of a third person, "The Lord is about to come,"—and they are introduced into an apartment with a low ceiling and no furniture. What strikes him at first is, opposite him, a long chrysalis of the colour of blood, with a man's head, from which rays escape, and the word Knouphis written in Greek all around. It rises above a shaft of a column placed in the midst of a pedestal. On the other walls of the apartment, medallions of polished brass represent heads of animals—that of an ox, of a lion, of an eagle, of a dog, and again, an ass's head! The argil lamps, suspended below these images, shed a flickering light. Antony, through a hole in the wall, perceives the moon, which shines far away on the waves, and he can even distinguish their monotonous ripple, with the dull sound of a ship's keel striking against the stones of a pier.

Men, squatting on the ground, their faces hidden beneath their cloaks, give vent at intervals to a kind of stifled barking. Women are sleeping, with their foreheads clasped by both arms, which are supported by their knees, so completely shrouded by their veils that one would say they were heaps of clothes arranged along the wall. Beside them, children, half-naked, and half devoured with vermin, watch the lamps burning, with an idiotic air;—and they are doing nothing; they are awaiting something.

They speak in low voices about their families, or communicate to one another remedies for their diseases. Many of them are going to embark at the end of the day, the persecution having become too severe. The Pagans, however, are not hard to deceive. "They believe, the fools, that we adore Knouphis!"

But one of the brethren, suddenly inspired, places himself in front of the column, where they have laid a loaf of bread, which is on the top of a basket full of fennel and hartwort.

The others have taken their places, forming, as they stand, three parallel lines.

The inspired one unrolls a paper covered with cylinders joined together, and then begins:

"Upon the darkness the ray of the Word descended, and a violent cry burst forth, which seemed like the voice of light."

All responding, while they sway their bodies to and fro:

"Kyrie eleison!"

The inspired one—"Man, then, was created by the infamous God of Israel, with the assistance of those here,"—pointing towards the medallions—"Aristophaios, Oraios, Sabaoth, Adonai, Eloi and Iaô!

"And he lay on the mud, hideous, feeble, shapeless, without the power of thought."

All, in a plaintive tone:

"Kyrie eleison!"

The inspired one—"But Sophia, taking pity on him, quickened him with a portion of her spirit. Then, seeing man so beautiful, God was seized with anger, and imprisoned him in His kingdom, interdicting him from the tree of knowledge. Still, once more, the other one came to his aid. She sent the serpent, who, with its sinuous advances, prevailed on him to disobey this law of hate. And man, when he had tasted knowledge, understood heavenly matters."

All, with energy:

"Kyrie eleison!"

The inspired one—"But Jaldalaoth, in order to be revenged, plunged man into matter, and the serpent along with him!"

All, in very low tones:

"Kyrie eleison!"

59

They close their mouths and then become silent.

The odours of the harbour mingle in the warm air with the smoke of the lamps. Their wicks, spluttering, are on the point of being extinguished, and long mosquitoes flutter around them. Antony gasps with anguish. He has the feeling that some monstrosity is floating around him—the horror of a crime about to be perpetrated.

But the inspired one, stamping with his feet, snapping his fingers, tossing his head, sings a psalm, with a wild refrain, to the sound of cymbals and of a shrill flute:

"Come! come! come! come forth from thy cavern!

"Swift One, that runs without feet, captor that takes without hands! Sinuous as the waves, round as the sun, darkened with spots of gold; like the firmament, strewn with stars! like the twistings of the vine-tree and the windings of entrails!

"Unbegotten! earth-devourer! ever young! perspicacious! honoured at Epidaurus! good for men! who cured King Ptolemy, the soldiers of Moses, and Glaucus, son of Minos!

"Come! come! come! come forth from thy cavern!"

All repeat:

"Come! come! come! come forth from thy cavern!"

However, there is no manifestation.

"Why, what is the matter with him?"

They proceed to deliberate, and to make suggestions. One old man offers a clump of grass. Then there is a rising in the basket. The green herbs are agitated; the flowers fall, and the head of a python appears.

He passes slowly over the edge of the loaf, like a circle turning round a motionless disc; then he develops, lengthens; he becomes

60

of enormous weight. To prevent him from grazing the ground, the men support him with their breasts, the women with their heads, and the children with the tips of their fingers; and his tail, emerging through the hole in the wall, stretches out indefinitely, even to the depths of the sea. His rings unfold themselves, and fill the apartment. They wind themselves round Antony.

The Faithful, pressing their mouths against his skin, snatch the bread which he has nibbled.

"It is thou! it is thou!

"Raised at first by Moses, crushed by Ezechias, re-established by the Messiah. He drank thee in the waters of baptism; but thou didst quit him in the Garden of Olives, and then he felt all his weakness.

"Writhing on the bar of the Cross, and higher than his head, slavering above the crown of thorns, thou didst behold him dying; for thou art Jesus! yes, thou art the Word! thou art the Christ!"

Antony swoons in horror, and falls in his cell, upon the splinters of wood, where the torch, which had slipped from his hand, is burning mildly. This commotion causes him to half-open his eyes; and he perceives the Nile, undulating and clear, under the light of the moon, like a great serpent in the midst of the sands—so much so that the hallucination again takes possession of him. He has not quitted the Ophites; they surround him, address him by name, carry off baggages, and descend towards the port. He embarks along with them.

A brief period of time flows by. Then the vault of a prison encircles him. In front of him, iron bars make black lines upon a background of blue; and at its sides, in the shade, are people weeping and praying, surrounded by others who are exhorting and consoling them.

Without, one is attracted by the murmuring of a crowd, as well as by the splendour of a summer's day. Shrill voices are crying out watermelons, water, iced drinks, and cushions of grass to sit down on. From time to time, shouts of applause burst forth. He observes people walking on their heads.

Suddenly, comes a continuous roaring, strong and cavernous, like the noise of water in an aqueduct: and, opposite him, he perceives, behind the bars of another cage, a lion, who is walking up and down; then a row of sandals, of naked legs, and of purple fringes.

Overhead, groups of people, ranged symmetrically, widen out from the lowest circle, which encloses the arena, to the highest, where masts have been raised to support a veil of hyacinth hung in the air on ropes. Staircases, which radiate towards the centre, intersect, at equal distances, those great circles of stone. Their steps disappear from view, owing to the vast audience seated there—knights, senators, soldiers, common people, vestals and courtesans, in woollen hoods, in silk maniples, in tawny tunics with aigrettes of precious stones, tufts of feathers and lictors' rods; and all this assemblage, muttering, exclaiming, tumultuous and frantic, stuns him like an immense tub boiling over. In the midst of the arena, upon an altar, smokes a vessel of incense.

The people who surround him are Christians, delivered up to the wild beasts. The men wear the red cloak of the high-priests of Saturn, the women the fillets of Ceres. Their friends distribute fragments of their garments and rings. In order to gain admittance into the prison, they require, they say, a great deal of money; but what does it matter? They will remain till the end.

Amongst these consolers Antony observes a bald man in a black tunic, a portion of whose face is plainly visible. He discourses with them on the nothingness of the world, and the happiness of the Elect. Antony is filled with transports of Divine love. He longs for the opportunity of sacrificing his life for the Saviour, not knowing whether he is himself one of these martyrs. But, save a Phrygian, with long hair, who keeps his arms raised, they all have a melancholy aspect. An old man is sobbing on a bench, and a young man, who is standing, is musing with downcast eyes.

The old man has refused to pay tribute at the angle of a cross-road, before a statue of Minerva; and he regards his companions with a look which signifies:

"You ought to succour me! Communities sometimes make arrangements by which they might be left in peace. Many amongst you have even obtained letters falsely declaring that you have offered sacrifice to idols."

He asks:

"Is it not Peter of Alexandria who has regulated what one ought to do when one is overcome by tortures?"

Then, to himself:

"Ah! this is very hard at my age! my infirmities render me so feeble! Perchance, I might have lived to another winter!"

The recollection of his little garden moves him to tears; and he contemplates the side of the altar.

The young man, who had disturbed by violence a feast of Apollo, murmurs:

"My only chance was to fly to the mountains!"

"The soldiers would have caught you," says one of the brethren.

"Oh! I could have done like Cyprian; I should have come back; and the second time I should have had more strength, you may be sure!"

Then he thinks of the countless days he should have lived, with all the pleasures which he will not have known;—and he, likewise, contemplates the side of the altar.

But the man in the black tunic rushes up to him:

"How scandalous! What? You a victim of election? Think of all these women who are looking at you! And then, God sometimes performs a miracle. Pionius benumbed the hands of his executioners; and the blood of Polycarp extinguished the flames of his funeral-pile."

He turns towards the old man. "Father, father! You ought to edify us by your death. By deferring it, you will, without doubt, commit some bad action which will destroy the fruit of your good deeds. Besides, the power of God is infinite. Perhaps your example will convert the entire people."

And, in the den opposite, the lions stride up and down, without stopping, rapidly, with a continuous movement. The largest of them all at once fixes his eyes on Antony and emits a roar, and a mass of vapour issues from his jaws.

The women are jammed up against the men.

The consoler goes from one to another:

"What would ye say—what would any of you say—if they burned you with plates of iron; if horses tore you asunder; if your body, coated with honey, was devoured by insects? You will have only the death of a hunter who is surprised in a wood."

Antony would much prefer all this than the horrible wild beasts; he imagines he feels their teeth and their talons, and that he hears his back cracking under their jaws.

A belluarius enters the dungeon; the martyrs tremble. One alone amongst them is unmoved—the Phrygian, who has gone into a corner to pray. He had burned three temples. He now advances with lifted arms, open mouth, and his head towards Heaven, without seeing anything, like a somnambulist.

The consoler exclaims:

"Keep back! Keep back! The Spirit of Montanus will destroy ye!"

All fall back, vociferating:

"Damnation to the Montanist!"

They insult him, spit upon him, would like to strike him. The lions, prancing, bite one another's manes. The people yell:

"To the beasts! To the beasts!"

The martyrs, bursting into sobs, catch hold of one another. A cup of narcotic wine is offered to them. They quickly pass it from hand to hand.

Near the door of the den another belluarius awaits the signal. It opens; a lion comes out.

He crosses the arena with great irregular strides. Behind him in a row appear the other lions, then a bear, three panthers, and leopards. They scatter like a flock in a prairie.

The cracking of a whip is heard. The Christians stagger, and, in order to make an end of it, their brethren push them forward.

Antony closes his eyes.

He opens them again. But darkness envelops him. Ere long, it grows bright once more; and he is able to trace the outlines of a plain, arid and covered with knolls, such as may be seen around a deserted quarry. Here and there a clump of shrubs lifts itself in the midst of the slabs, which are on a level with the soil, and above which white forms are bending, more undefined than clouds. Others rapidly make their appearance. Eyes shine through the openings of long veils. By their indolent gait and the perfumes which exhale from them, Antony knows they are ladies of patrician rank. There are also men, but of inferior condition, for they have visages at the same time simple and coarse.

One of the women, with a long breath:

"Ah! how pleasant is the air of the chilly night in the midst of sepulchres! I am so fatigued with the softness of couches, the noise of day, and the oppressiveness of the sun!"

A woman, panting—"Ah! at last, here I am! But how irksome to have wedded an idolater!"

Another—"The visits to the prisons, the conversations with our brethren, all excite the suspicions of our husbands! And we must even hide ourselves from them when making the sign of the Cross; they would take it for a magical conjuration."

Another—"With mine, there was nothing but quarrelling all day long. I did not like to submit to the abuses to which he subjected my person; and, for revenge, he had me persecuted as a Christian."

Another—"Recall to your memory that young man of such striking beauty who was dragged by the heels behind a chariot, like Hector, from the Esquiline Gate to the Mountains of Tibur; and his blood stained the bushes on both sides of the road. I collected the drops— here they are!"

She draws from her bosom a sponge perfectly black, covers it with kisses, and then flings herself upon the slab, crying:

"Ah! my friend! my friend!"

A man—"It is just three years to-day since Domitilla's death. She was stoned at the bottom of the Wood of Proserpine. I gathered her bones, which shone like glow-worms in the grass. The earth now covers them."

He flings himself upon a tombstone.

"O my betrothed! my betrothed!"

And all the others, scattered through the plain:

"O my sister!" "O my brother!" "O my daughter!" "O my mother!"

They are on their knees, their foreheads clasped with their hands, or their bodies lying flat with both arms extended; and the sobs which they repress make their bosoms swell almost to bursting. They gaze up at the sky, saying:

66

"Have pity on her soul, O my God! She is languishing in the abode of shadows. Deign to admit her into the Resurrection, so that she may rejoice in Thy light!"

Or, with eyes fixed on the flagstones, they murmur:

"Be at rest—suffer no more! I have brought thee wine and meat!"

A widow—"Here is pudding, made by me, according to his taste, with many eggs, and a double measure of flour. We are going to eat together as of yore, is not that so?"

She puts a little of it on her lips, and suddenly begins to laugh in an extravagant fashion, frantically.

The others, like her, nibble a morsel and drink a mouthful; they tell one another the history of their martyrs; their sorrow becomes vehement; their libations increase; their eyes, swimming with tears, are fixed on one another; they stammer with inebriety and desolation. Gradually their hands touch; their lips meet; their veils are torn away, and they embrace one another upon the tombs in the midst of the cups and the torches.

The sky begins to brighten. The mist soaks their garments; and, as if they were strangers to one another, they take their departure by different roads into the country.

The sun shines forth. The grass has grown taller; the plain has become transformed. Across the bamboos, Antony sees a forest of columns of a bluish-grey colour. Those are trunks of trees springing from a single trunk. From each of its branches descend other branches which penetrate into the soil; and the whole of those horizontal and perpendicular lines, indefinitely multiplied, might be compared to a gigantic framework were it not that here and there appears a little fig-tree with a dark foliage like that of a sycamore. Between the branches he distinguishes bunches of yellow flowers and violets, and ferns as large as birds' feathers. Under the lowest branches may be seen at different points the horns of a buffalo, or the glittering eyes of an antelope. Parrots sit perched, butterflies flutter, lizards crawl upon the ground, flies buzz; and one can hear, as it were, in the midst of the silence, the palpitation of an all-permeating life.

At the entrance of the wood, on a kind of pile, is a strange sight—a man coated over with cows' dung, completely naked, more dried-up than a mummy. His joints form knots at the extremities of his bones, which are like sticks. He has clusters of shells in his ears, his face is very long, and his nose is like a vulture's beak. His left arm is held erect in the air, crooked, and stiff as a stake; and he has remained there so long that birds have made a nest in his hair.

At the four corners of his pile four fires are blazing. The sun is right in his face. He gazes at it with great open eyes, and without looking at Antony.

"Brahmin of the banks of the Nile, what sayest thou?"

Flames start out on every side through the partings of the beams; and the gymnosophist resumes:

"Like a rhinoceros, I am plunged in solitude. I dwelt in the tree that was behind me."

In fact, the large fig-tree presents in its flutings a natural excavation of the shape of a man.

"And I fed myself on flowers and fruits with such an observance of precepts that not even a dog has seen me eat.

"As existence proceeds from corruption, corruption from desire, desire from sensation, and sensation from contact, I have avoided every kind of action, every kind of contact, and—without stirring any more than the pillar of a tombstone—exhaling my breath through my two nostrils, fixing my glances upon my nose; and, observing the ether in my spirit, the world in my limbs, the moon in my heart, I pondered on the essence of the great soul, whence continually escape, like sparks of fire, the principles of life. I have, at last, grasped the supreme soul in all beings, all beings in the supreme soul; and I have succeeded in making my soul penetrate the place into which my senses used to penetrate.

"I receive knowledge directly from Heaven, like the bird Tchataka, who quenches his thirst only in the droppings of the rain. From the very fact of my having knowledge of things, things no longer exist. For me now there is no hope and no anguish, no goodness, no virtue, neither day nor night, neither thou nor I—absolutely nothing.

"My frightful austerities have made me superior to the Powers. A contraction of my brain can kill a hundred kings' sons, dethrone gods, overrun the world."

He utters all this in a monotonous voice. The leaves all around him are withered. The rats fly over the ground.

He slowly lowers his eyes towards the flames, which are rising, then adds:

"I have become disgusted with form, disgusted with perception, disgusted even with knowledge itself—for thought does not outlive the transitory fact that gives rise to it; and the spirit, like the rest, is but an illusion.

"Everything that is born will perish; everything that is dead will come to life again. The beings that have actually disappeared will sojourn in wombs not yet formed, and will come back to earth to serve with sorrow other creatures. But, as I have resolved through an infinite number of existences, under the guise of gods, men, and animals, I give up travelling, and no longer wish for this fatigue. I abandon the dirty inn of my body, walled in with flesh, reddened with blood, covered with hideous skin, full of uncleanness; and, for my reward, I shall, finally, sleep in the very depths of the absolute, in annihilation."

The flames rise to his breast, then envelop him. His head stretches across as if through the hole of a wall. His eyes are perpetually fixed in a vacant stare.

Antony gets up again. The torch on the ground has set fire to the splinters of wood, and the flames have singed his beard. Bursting into an exclamation, Antony tramples on the fire; and, when only a heap of cinders is left:

"Where, then, is Hilarion? He was here just now. I saw him! Ah! no; it is impossible! I am mistaken! How is this? My cell, those stones, the sand, have not, perhaps, any more reality. I must be going mad. Stay! where was I? What was happening here?

"Ah! the gymnosophist! This death is common amongst the Indian sages. Kalanos burned himself before Alexander; another did the same in the time of Augustus. What hatred of life they must have had!—unless, indeed, pride drove them to it. No matter, it is the intrepidity of martyrs! As to the others, I now believe all that has been told me of the excesses they have occasioned.

"And before this? Yes, I recollect! the crowd of heresiarchs ... What shrieks! what eyes! But why so many outbreaks of the flesh and wanderings of the spirit?

"It is towards God they pretend to direct their thoughts in all these different ways. What right have I to curse them, I who stumble in my own path? When they have disappeared, I shall, perhaps, learn more. This one rushed away too quickly; I had not time to reply to him. Just now it is as if I had in my intellect more space and more light. I am tranquil. I feel myself capable ... But what is this now? I thought I had extinguished the fire."

A flame flutters between the rocks; and, speedily, a jerky voice makes itself heard from the mountains in the distance.

"Are those the barkings of a hyena, or the lamentations of some lost traveller?"

Antony listens. The flame draws nearer.

70

And he sees approaching a woman who is weeping, resting on the shoulder of a man with a white beard. She is covered with a purple garment all in rags. He, like her, is bare-headed, with a tunic of the same colour, and carries a bronze vase, whence arises a small blue flame.

Antony is filled with fear,—and yet he would fain know who this woman is.

The stranger (Simon)—"This is a young girl, a poor child, whom I take everywhere with me."

He raises the bronze vase. Antony inspects her by the light of this flickering flame. She has on her face marks of bites, and traces of blows along her arms. Her scattered hair is entangled in the rents of her rags; her eyes appear insensible to the light.

Simon—"Sometimes she remains thus a long time without speaking or eating, and utters marvellous things."

Antony—"Really?"

Simon—"Eunoia! Eunoia! relate what you have to say!"

She turns around her eyeballs, as if awakening from a dream, passes her fingers slowly across her two lids, and in a mournful voice:

Helena (Eunoia)—"I have a recollection of a distant region, of the colour of emerald. There is only a single tree there."

Antony gives a start.

"At each step of its huge branches a pair of spirits stand. The branches around them cross each other, like the veins of a body, and they watch the eternal life circulating from the roots, where it is lost in shadow up to the summit, which reaches beyond the sun. I, on the second branch, illumined with my face the summer nights."

Antony, touching his forehead—"Ah! ah! I understand! the head!"

Simon, with his finger on his lips—"Hush! Hush!"

Helena—"The vessel remained convex: her keel clave the foam. He said to me, 'What does it matter if I disturb my country, if I lose my kingdom! You will be mine, in my own house!'

"How pleasant was the upper chamber of his palace! He would lie down upon the ivory bed, and, smoothing my hair, would sing in an amorous strain. At the end of the day, I could see the two camps and the lanterns which they were lighting; Ulysses at the edge of his tent; Achilles, armed from head to foot, driving a chariot along the seashore."

Antony—"Why, she is quite mad! Wherefore? ..."

Simon—"Hush! Hush!"

Helena—"They rubbed me with unguents, and sold me to the people to amuse them. One evening, standing with the sistrum in my hand, I was coaxing Greek sailors to dance. The rain, like a cataract, fell upon the tavern, and the cups of hot wine were smoking. A man entered without the door having been opened."

Simon—"It was I! I found you. Here she is, Antony; she who is called Sigeh, Eunoia, Barbelo, Prounikos! The Spirits who govern the world were jealous of her, and they bound her in the body of a woman. She was the Helen of the Trojans, whose memory the poet Stesichorus had rendered infamous. She has been Lucretia, the patrician lady violated by the kings. She was Delilah, who cut off the hair of Samson. She was that daughter of Israel who surrendered herself to he-goats. She has loved adultery, idolatry, lying and folly. She was prostituted by every nation. She has sung in all the cross-ways. She has kissed every face. At Tyre, she, the Syrian, was the mistress of thieves. She drank with them during the nights, and she concealed assassins amid the vermin of her tepid bed."

Antony—"Ah! what is coming over me?"

Simon, with a furious air —

"I have redeemed her, I tell you, and re-established her in all her splendour, such as Caius Cæsar Agricola became enamoured of when he desired to sleep with the Moon!"

Antony—-"Well! well!"

Simon—"But she really is the Moon! Has not Pope Clement written that she was imprisoned in a tower? Three hundred persons came to surround the tower; and on each of the murderers, at the same time, the moon was seen to appear,—though there are not many moons in the world, or many Eunoias!"

Antony—"Yes! ... I think I recollect ..."

And he falls into a reverie.

Simon—"Innocent as Christ, who died for men, she has devoted herself to women. For the powerlessness of Jehovah is demonstrated by the transgression of Adam, and we must shake off the old law, opposed, as it is, to the order of things. I have preached the new Gospel in Ephraim and in Issachar, along the torrent of Bizor, behind the lake of Houleh, in the valley of Mageddo, and beyond the mountains, at Bostra and at Damas. Let those who are covered with wine-dregs, those who are covered with dirt, those who are covered with blood, come to me; and I will wash out their defilement with the Holy Spirit, called by the Greeks, Minerva. She is Minerva! She is the Holy Spirit! I am Jupiter Apollo, the Christ, the Paraclete, the great power of God incarnated in the person of Simon!"

Antony—"Ah! it is you! ... it is you! But I know your crimes! You were born at Gittha on the borders of Samaria. Dositheus, your first master, dismissed you! You execrate Saint Paul for having converted one of your women; and, vanquished by Saint Peter, in your rage and terror, you flung into the waves the bag which contained your magical instruments!"

Simon—"Do you desire them?"

Antony looks at him, and an inner voice murmurs in his breast, "Why not?"

Simon resumes:

"He who understands the powers of Nature and the substance of spirits ought to perform miracles. It is the dream of all sages—and the desire of which gnaws you; confess it!

"Amongst the Romans I flew so high in the circus that they saw me no more. Nero ordered me to be decapitated; but it was a sheep's head that fell to the ground instead of mine. Finally, they buried me alive; but I came back to life on the third day. The proof of it is that I am here!"

He gives him his hands to smell. They have the odour of a corpse. Antony recoils.

"I can make bronze serpents move, marble statues laugh, and dogs speak. I will show you an immense quantity of gold, I will set up kings, you shall see nations adoring me. I can walk on the clouds and on the waves; pass through mountains; assume the appearance of a young man, or of an old man; of a tiger, or of an ant; take your face, give you mine; and drive the thunderbolt. Do you hear?"

The thunder rolls, followed by flashes of lightning.

"It is the voice of the Most High, 'for the Eternal, thy God, is a fire,' and all creations operate by the emanations of this central fire. You are about to receive the baptism of it—that second baptism, announced by Jesus, which fell on the Apostles one stormy day when the window was open!"

And all the while stirring the flame with his hand, slowly, as if to sprinkle Antony with it:

"Mother of Mercies, thou who discoverest secrets in order that we may have rest in the eighth house ..."

74

Antony exclaims:

"Ah! if I had holy water!"

The flame goes out, producing much smoke.

Eunoia and Simon have disappeared.

An extremely cold fog, opaque and f[oe]tid, fills the atmosphere.

Antony, extending his arms like a blind man—

"Where am I? ... I am afraid of falling into the abyss. And the cross, no doubt, is too far away from me. Ah! what a night! what a night!"

A sudden gust of wind cleaves the fog asunder; and he perceives two men covered with long white tunics. The first is of tall stature, with a sweet expression of countenance and grave deportment. His white hair, parted like that of Christ, descends regularly over his shoulders. He has thrown down a wand which he was carrying in his hand, and which his companion has taken up, making a respectful bow after the fashion of Orientals. The other is small, coarse-looking, flat-nosed, with a thick neck, curly hair, and an air of simplicity. Both of them are bare-footed, bare-headed, and covered with dust, like people who have come on a long journey.

Antony, with a start—"What do ye seek? Speak! Go on!"

Damis—He is the little man—

"La, la! ... worthy hermit! what do you say? I know nothing about it. Here is the Master!"

He sits down; the other remains standing. Silence.

Antony, resumes—"Ye come in this fashion? ..."

Damis—"Oh! a great distance—a very great distance!"

Antony—"And ye are going? ..."

75

Damis, pointing at his companion—"Wherever he wishes."

Antony—"Who, then, is he?"

Damis—"Look at him."

Antony—"He has the appearance of a saint. If I dared ..."

The fog by this time is quite gone. The atmosphere has become perfectly clear. The moon shines out.

Damis—"What are you thinking of now that you say nothing more?"

Antony—"I am thinking of——Oh! nothing."

Damis draws close to Apollonius, makes many turns round him, with his figure bent, and without moving his head.

"Master, this is a Galilean hermit who wishes to know the sources of your wisdom."

Apollonius—"Let him approach."

Antony hesitates.

Damis—"Approach!"

Apollonius, in a voice of thunder—

"Approach! You would like to know who I am, what I have done, what I am thinking of? Is that not so, child?"

Antony—" ... If at the same time those things contribute to my salvation."

Apollonius—"Rejoice! I am about to tell them to you!"

Damis, in a low tone to Antony—

"Is it possible? He must have, at the first glance, recognised your extraordinary inclinations for philosophy! I shall profit by it also myself."

Apollonius—"I will first describe to you the long road I travelled to gain doctrine; and, if you find in all my life one bad action, you will stop me—for he must scandalise by his words who has offended by his actions."

Damis to Antony:

"What a just man! eh?"

Antony—"Decidedly, I believe he is sincere."

Apollonius—"The night of my birth, my mother thought she saw herself gathering flowers on the border of a lake. A flash of lightning appeared; and she brought me into the world amid the cries of swans who were singing in her dream. Up to my fifteenth year, they plunged me three times a day into the fountain Asbadeus, whose waters render perjurers dropsical; and they rubbed my body with leaves of cnyza, to make me chaste. A princess from Palmyra sought me out, one evening, and offered me treasures, which she knew were hidden in tombs. A priest of the temple of Diana cut his throat in despair with the sacrificial knife; and the Governor of Cilicia, after repeated promises, declared before my family that he would put me to death; but it was he who died three days after, assassinated by the Romans."

Damis, to Antony, striking him on the elbow—"Eh? Just as I told you! What a man!"

Apollonius—"I have for four years in succession observed the complete silence of the Pythagoreans. The most unforeseen calamity did not draw one sigh from me; and, at the theatre, when I entered, they turned aside from me as from a phantom."

Damis—"Would you have done that—you?"

Apollonius—"The time of my ordeal ended, I undertook to instruct the priests who had lost the tradition."

77

Antony—"What tradition?"

Damis—"Let him continue. Be silent!"

Apollonius—"I have conversed with the Samaneans of the Ganges, with the astrologers of Chaldea, with the magi of Babylon, with the Gaulish druids, with the priests of the negroes. I have climbed the fourteen Olympi; I have sounded the Lakes of Sythia; I have measured the vastness of the desert!"

Damis—"All this is undoubtedly true. I was there myself!"

Apollonius—"At first, I went as far as the Hyrcanian Sea. I have gone all round it, and through the country of the Baraomatæ, where Bucephalus is buried. I have gone down to Nineveh. At the gates of the city a man came up to me."

Damis—"I! I! my good Master! I loved you from the very beginning. You were sweeter than a girl, and more beautiful than a god!"

Appollonius, without listening to him—"He wished to accompany me, in order to act as an interpreter for me."

Damis—"But you replied that you understood every language, and that you divined all thoughts. Then I kissed the end of your mantle, and I walked behind you."

Apollonius—"After Ctesiphon, we entered into the land of Babylon."

Damis—"And the satrap uttered an exclamation on seeing a man so pale."

Antony, to himself—"Which signifies——?"

Apollonius—"The King received me standing near a throne of silver, in a circular hall studded with stars, and from a cupola hung, from unseen threads, four great golden birds, with both wings extended."

Antony, musing—"Are there such things on the earth?"

Damis—"That is, indeed, a city—Babylon! Everyone is rich there! The houses, painted blue, have gates of bronze, with staircases that lead down to the river."

Making a sketch with his stick on the ground:

"Like that, do you see? And then there are temples, squares, baths, aqueducts! The palaces are covered with copper! and then the interior, if you only saw it!"

Apollonius—"On the northern wall rises a tower, which supports a second, a third, a fourth, a fifth; and there are three others besides! The eighth is a chapel with a bed in it. Nobody enters there but the woman chosen by the priests for the God Belus. The King of Babylon made me take up my quarters in it."

Damis—"They scarcely paid any heed to me. I was left, too, to walk about the streets by myself. I enquired into the customs of the people; I visited the workshops; I examined the huge machines which bring water into the gardens. But it annoyed me to be separated from the Master."

Apollonius—"At last, we left Babylon; and, by the light of the moon, we suddenly saw a wild mare."

Damis—"Yes, indeed! she sprang forth on her iron hoofs; she neighed like an ass; she galloped amongst the rocks. He burst into angry abuse of her; and she disappeared."

Antony, aside—"Where can they have come from?"

Apollonius—"At Taxilla, capital of five thousand fortresses, Phraortes, King of the Ganges, showed us his guard of tall black men, five cubits high, and in the gardens of his palace, under a pavilion of green brocade, an enormous elephant, whom the queens used to amuse themselves in perfuming. This was the elephant of Porus, who fled after the death of Alexander."

Damis—"And which was found again in a forest."

Antony—"They talk a great deal, like drunken people."

Apollonius—"Phraortes made us sit down at his table."

Damis—"What an odd country! The noblemen, while drinking, amuse themselves by flinging arrows under the feet of a child who is dancing. But I do not approve ..."

Apollonius—"When I was ready to depart, the King gave me a parasol, and said to me: 'I have, on the Indus, a stud of white camels. When you do not want them any longer, blow into their ears, and they will return.' We proceeded along the river, walking in the night by the gleaming of the glow-worms, who emitted their radiance through the bamboos. The slave whistled an air to keep off the serpents; and our camels bent the reins while passing under the trees, as if under doors that were too low. One day, a black child, who held in his hand a caduceus of gold, conducted us to the College of Sages. Iarchas, their chief, spoke to me of my ancestors, of all my thoughts, of all my actions, and all my existences. He had been the river Indus, and he recalled to my mind that I had conducted the boats on the Nile in the time of King Sesostris."

Damis—"As for me, they told me nothing, so that I do not know what I was."

Antony—"They have the unsubstantial air of shadows."

Apollonius—"We met on the seashore the cynocephali, glutted with milk, who were returning from their expedition in the Island of Taprobane. The tepid waves pushed white pearls before us. The amber cracked under our footsteps. Whales' skeletons were bleaching in the crevices of the cliffs. In short, the earth grew more contracted than a sandal;—and, after casting towards the sun drops from the ocean, we turned to the right to go back. We returned through the region of the Aromatæ, through the country of the Gangaridæ, the promontory of Comaria, the land of the Sachalitæ, of the Aramitæ, and the Homeritæ; then across the Cassanian mountains, the Red Sea, and the Island of Topazes, we penetrated into Ethiopia, through the kingdom of the Pygmæi."

Antony, aside—"How large the earth is!"

Damis—"And when we got home again, all those whom we had known in former days were dead."

Antony hangs his head. Silence.

Apollonius goes on:

"Then they began talking about me in the world. The plague ravaged Ephesus; I made them stone an old mendicant."

Damis—"And the plague was gone!"

Antony—"What! He banishes diseases?"

Apollonius—"At Cnidus, I cured the lover of Venus."

Damis—"Yes, a madman, who had even promised to marry her. To love a woman is bad enough; but a statue—what idiocy! The Master placed his hand on this man's heart, and immediately the love was extinguished."

Antony—"What! He drives out demons?"

Apollonius—"At Tarentum, they brought to the stake a young girl who was dead."

Damis—"The Master touched her lips; and she arose, calling on her mother."

Antony—"Can it be? He brings the dead back to life?"

Apollonius—"I foretold that Vespasian would be Emperor."

Antony—"What! He divines the future?"

Damis—"There was at Corinth——"

Apollonius—"While I was supping with him at the waters of Baia-"

Antony—"Excuse me, strangers; it is late!"

Damis—"——A young man named Menippus."

Antony—"No! no! go away!"

Apollonius—"——A dog entered, carrying in its mouth a hand that had been cut off."

Damis—"——One evening, in one of the suburbs, he met a woman."

Antony—"You do not hear me. Take yourselves off!"

Damis—"——He prowled vacantly around the couches."

Antony—"Enough!"

Apollonius—"——They wanted to drive him away."

Damis—"——Menippus, then, surrendered himself to her; and they became lovers."

Apollonius—"——And, beating the mosaic floor with his tail, he deposited this hand on the knees of Flavius."

Damis—"——But, in the morning, at the school-lectures, Menippus was pale."

Antony, with a bound—"Still at it! Well, let them go on, since there is not ..."

Damis—"The Master said to him: 'O beautiful young man, you are caressing a serpent; and a serpent is caressing you. For how long are these nuptials?' Every one of us went to the wedding."

Antony—"I am doing wrong, surely, in listening to this!"

Damis—"Servants were busily engaged at the vestibule; the doors flew open; nevertheless, one could hear neither the noise of footsteps, nor the sound of opening doors. The Master seated himself beside Menippus. Immediately, the bride was seized with anger against the philosophers. But the vessels of gold, the cup-bearers, the cooks, the attendants, disappeared; the roof flew away; the walls fell in; and Apollonius remained alone, standing with this woman all in tears at his feet. It was a vampire, who satisfied the handsome young men in order to devour their flesh—because nothing is better for phantoms of this kind than the blood of lovers."

Apollonius—"If you wish to know the art— —"

Antony—"I wish to know nothing."

Apollonius—"On the evening of our arrival at the gates of Rome— —"

Antony—"Oh! yes, tell me about the City of the Popes."

Apollonius—"— —A drunken man accosted us who sang with a sweet voice. It was an epithalamium of Nero; and he had the power of causing the death of anyone who heard him with indifference. He carried on his back in a box a string taken from the cithara of the Emperor. I shrugged my shoulders. He threw mud in our faces. Then I unfastened my girdle and placed it in his hands."

Damis—"In this instance you were quite wrong!"

Apollonius—"The Emperor, during the night, made me call at his residence. He played at ossicles with Sporus, leaning with his left arm on a table of agate. He turned round, and, knitting his fair brows: 'Why are you not afraid of me?' he asked. 'Because the God who made you terrible has made me intrepid,' I replied."

Antony, to himself—"Something unaccountable fills me with fear."

Silence.

Damis resumes, in a shrill voice—"All Asia, moreover, could tell you ..."

Antony, starting up—"I am sick. Leave me!"

Damis—"Listen now. At Ephesus, he witnessed the death of Domitian, who was at Rome."

Antony making an effort to laugh—"Is this possible?"

Damis—"Yes, at the theatre, in broad daylight, on the fourteenth of the Kalends of October, he suddenly exclaimed: 'They are murdering Cæsar!' and he added, every now and then, 'He rolls on the ground! Oh! how he struggles! He gets up again; he attempts to fly; the gates are shut. Ah! it is finished. He is dead!' And that very day, in fact, Titus Flavius Domitianus was assassinated, as you are aware."

Antony—"Without the aid of the Devil ... No doubt ..."

Apollonius—"He wished to put me to death, this Domitian. Damis fled by my direction, and I remained alone in my prison."

Damis—"It was a terrible bit of daring, I must confess!"

Apollonius—"About the fifth hour, the soldiers led me to the tribunal. I had my speech quite ready, which I kept under my cloak."

Damis—"The rest of us were on the bank of Puzzoli! We saw you die; we wept; when, towards the sixth hour, all at once, you appeared, and said to us, 'It is I.'"

Antony, aside—"Just like Him!"

Damis, very loudly—"Absolutely!"

Antony—"Oh, no! you are lying, are you not? You are lying!"

Apollonius—"He came down from Heaven—I ascend there, thanks to my virtue, which has raised me even to the height of the Most High!"

Damis—"Tyana, his native city, has erected a temple with priests in his honour!"

84

Apollonius draws close to Antony, and, bending towards his ear, says:

"The truth is, I know all the gods, all the rites, all the prayers, all the oracles. I have penetrated into the cavern of Trophonius, the son of Apollo. I have moulded for the Syracusans the cakes which they use on the mountains. I have undergone the eighty tests of Mithra. I have pressed against my heart the serpent of Sabacius. I have received the scarf of the Cabiri. I have bathed Cybele in the waves of the Campanian Gulf; and I have passed three moons in the caverns of Samothrace!"

Damis, laughing stupidly—"Ah! ah! ah! at the mysteries of the Bona Dea!"

Apollonius—"And now we are renewing our pilgrimage. We are going to the North, the side of the swans and the snows. On the white plain the blind hippopodes break with the ends of their feet the ultramarine plant."

Damis—"Come! it is morning! The cock has crowed; the horse has neighed; the ship is ready."

Antony—"The cock has not crowed. I hear the cricket in the sands, and I see the moon, which remains in its place."

Apollonius—"We are going to the South, behind the mountains and the huge waves, to seek in the perfumes for the cause of love. You shall inhale the odour of myrrhodion, which makes the weak die. You shall bathe your body in the lake of pink oil of the Island of Juno. You shall see sleeping under the primroses the lizard who awakens all the centuries when at his maturity the carbuncle falls from his forehead. The stars glitter like eyes, the cascades sing like lyres, an intoxicating fragrance arises from the opening flowers. Your spirit shall expand in this atmosphere, and it will show itself in your heart as well as in your face."

Damis—"Master, it is time! The wind is about to rise; the swallows are awakening; the myrtle-leaf is shed."

Apollonius—"Yes, let us go!"

Antony—"No—not I! I remain!"

Apollonius—"Do you wish me to show you the plant Balis, which resuscitates the dead?"

Damis—"Ask him rather for the bloodstone, which attracts silver, iron and bronze!"

Antony—"Oh! how sick I feel! how sick I feel!"

Damis—"You shall understand the voices of all creatures, the roarings, the cooings!"

Apollonius—"I will make you mount the unicorns, the dragons, and the dolphins!"

Antony, weeps—"Oh! oh! oh!"

Apollonius—"You shall know the demons who dwell in the caverns, those who speak in the woods, those who move about in the waves, those who drive the clouds."

Damis—"Fasten your girdle! tie your sandals!"

Apollonius—"I will explain to you the reasons for the shapes of divinities; why it is that Apollo is upright, Jupiter sitting down, Venus black at Corinth, square at Athens, conical at Paphos."

Antony, clasping his hands—"I wish they would go away! I wish they would go away!"

Apollonius—"I will snatch off before your eyes the armour of the Gods; we shall force the sanctuaries; I will make you violate the pythoness!"

Antony—"Help, Lord!"

He flings himself against the cross.

Apollonius—"What is your desire? your dream? There's barely time to think of it ..."

Antony—"Jesus, Jesus, come to my aid!"

Apollonius—"Do you wish me to make Jesus appear?"

Antony—"What? How?"

Apollonius—"It shall be He—and no other! He shall cast off His crown, and we shall speak together face to face!"

Damis, in a low tone—"Say what you wish for most! Say what you wish for most!"

Antony, at the foot of the cross, murmurs prayers. Damis continues to run around him with wheedling gestures.

"See, worthy hermit, dear Saint Antony! pure man, illustrious man! man who cannot be sufficiently praised! Do not be alarmed; this is an exaggerated style of speaking, borrowed from the Orientals. It in no way prevents—"

Apollonius—"Let him alone, Damis! He believes, like a brute, in the reality of things. The fear which he has of the gods prevents him from comprehending them; and he eats his own words, just like a jealous king! But you, my son, quit me not!"

He steps back to the verge of the cliffs, passes over it and remains there, hanging in mid-air:

"Above all forms, farther than the earth, beyond the skies, dwells the World of Ideas, entirely filled with the Word. With one bound we leap across Space, and you shall grasp in its infinity the Eternal, the Absolute Being! Come! give me your hand. Let us go!"

The pair, side by side, rise softly into the air.

Antony, embracing the cross, watches them ascending.

They disappear.

CHAPTER V

All Gods, All Religions

ANTONY, walking slowly—"That was really Hell!

"Nebuchadnezzar did not dazzle me so much. The Queen of Sheba did not bewitch me so thoroughly. The way in which he spoke about the gods filled me with a longing to know them.

"I recollect having seen hundreds of them at a time, in the Island of Elephantinum, in the reign of Dioclesian. The Emperor had given up to the nomads a large territory, on condition that they should protect the frontiers; and the treaty was concluded in the name of the invisible Powers. For the gods of every people were ignorant about other people. The Barbarians had brought forward theirs. They occupied the hillocks of sand which line the river. One could see them holding their idols between their arms, like great paralytic children, or else, sailing amid cataracts on trunks of palm-trees, they pointed out from a distance the amulets on their necks and the tattooings on their breasts; and that is not more criminal than the religion of the Greeks, the Asiatics, and the Romans.

"When I dwelt in the Temple of Heliopolis, I used often to contemplate all the objects on the walls: vultures carrying sceptres, crocodiles playing on lyres, men's faces joined to serpents' bodies, women with cows' heads prostrated before the ithyphallic deities; and their supernatural forms carried me away into other worlds. I wished to know what those calm eyes were gazing at. In order that matter should have so much power, it should contain a spirit. The souls of the gods are attached to their images. Those who possess external beauty may fascinate us; but the others, who are abject or terrible ... how to believe in them? ..."

And he sees moving past, close to the ground, leaves, stones, shells, branches of trees, vague representations of animals, then a species of dropsical dwarfs. These are gods. He bursts out laughing.

Behind him, he hears another outburst of laughter; and Hilarion presents himself, dressed like a hermit, much bigger than before— in fact, colossal.

Antony is not surprised at seeing him again.

"What a brute one must be to adore a thing like that!"

Hilarion—"Oh! yes; very much of a brute!"

Then advance before them, one by one, idols of all nations and all ages, in wood, in metal, in granite, in feathers, and in skins sewn together. The oldest of them, anterior to the Deluge, are lost to view beneath the seaweed which hangs from them like hair. Some, too long for their lower portions, crack in their joints and break their loins while walking. Others allow sand to flow out through holes in their bellies.

Antony and Hilarion are prodigiously amused. They hold their sides from sheer laughter.

After this, idols pass with faces like sheep. They stagger on their bandy legs, open wide their eyelids, and bleat out, like dumb animals: "Ba! ba! ba!"

In proportion as they approach the human type, they irritate Antony the more. He strikes them with his fist, kicks them, rushes madly upon them. They begin to present a horrible aspect, with high tufts, eyes like bulls, arms terminated with claws, and the jaws of a shark. And, before these gods, men are slaughtered on altars of stone, while others are pounded in vats, crushed under chariot-wheels, or nailed to trees. There is one of them, all in red-hot iron, with the horns of a bull, who devours children.

Antony—"Horror!"

Hilarion—"But the gods always demand sufferings. Your own, even, has wished—"

Antony, weeping—"Say no more—hold your tongue!"

The enclosure of rocks changes into a valley. A herd of oxen pastures there on the shorn grass. The shepherd who has charge of them perceives a cloud; and in a sharp voice pierces the air with words of urgent entreaty.

Hilarion—"As he wants rain, he tries, by his strains, to coerce the King of Heaven to open the fruitful cloud."

Antony, laughing—"This is too silly a form of presumption!"

Hilarion—"Why, then, do you perform exorcisms?"

The valley becomes a sea of milk, motionless and illimitable.

In the midst of it floats a long cradle, formed by the coils of a serpent, all whose heads, bending forward at the same time, overshadow a god who lies there asleep. He is young, beardless, more beautiful than a girl, and covered with diaphanous veils. The pearls of his tiara shine softly, like moons; a chaplet of stars winds itself many times above his breast, and, with one hand under his head and the other arm extended, he reposes with a dreamy and intoxicated air. A woman squatted before his feet awaits his awakening.

Hilarion—"This is the primordial duality of the Brahmans—the absolute not expressing itself by any form."

Upon the navel of the god a stalk of lotus has grown; and in its calyx appears another god with three faces.

Antony—"Hold! what an invention!"

Hilarion—"Father, Son and Holy Ghost, in the same way make only one person!"

The three heads are turned aside, and three immense gods appear. The first, who is of a rosy hue, bites the end of his toe. The second, who is blue, tosses four arms about. The third, who is green, weaves a necklace of human skulls. Immediately in front of them rise three goddesses, one wrapped in a net, another offering a cup, and the third brandishing a bow.

And these gods, these goddesses multiply, become tenfold. On their shoulders rise arms, and at the ends of their arms are hands holding banners, axes, bucklers, swords, parasols and drums. Fountains spring from their heads, grass hangs from their nostrils.

Riding on birds, cradled on palanquins, throned on seats of gold, standing in niches of ivory, they dream, travel, command, drink wine and inhale flowers. Dancing-girls whirl around; giants pursue monsters; at the entrances to the grottoes, solitaries meditate. Myriads of stars and clouds of streamers mingle in an indistinguishable throng. Peacocks drink from the streams of golden dust. The embroidery of the pavilions blends with the spots of the leopards. Coloured rays cross one another in the blue air, amid the flying of arrows and the swinging of censers. And all this unfolds itself, like a lofty frieze, leaning with its base on the rocks and mounting to the very sky.

Antony, dazzled—"What a number of them there are! What do they wish?"

Hilarion—"The one who is scratching his abdomen with his elephant's trunk is the solar god, the inspirer of wisdom. That other, whose six heads carry towers and fourteen handles of javelins, is the prince of armies, the fire-devourer. The old man riding on a crocodile is going to bathe the souls of the dead on the seashore. They will be tormented by this black woman with rotten teeth, the governess of hell. The chariot drawn by red mares, which a legless coachman is driving, is carrying about in broad daylight the master of the sun. The moon-god accompanies him in a litter drawn by three gazelles. On her knees, on the back of a parrot, the goddess of beauty is presenting her round breast to Love, her son. Here she is farther on; she leaps with joy in the prairies. Look! look! With a radiant mitre on her head, she runs over the cornfields, over the waves, mounts into the air, and exhibits herself everywhere.

91

Between these gods sit the genii of the winds, of the planets, of the months, of the days, and a hundred thousand others! And their aspects are multiplied, their transformations rapid. Here is one who from a fish has become a tortoise, he assumes the head of a wild boar, the stature of a dwarf!"

Antony—"For what purpose?"

Hilarion—"To establish equilibrium, to combat evil. Life is exhausted, its forms are used up; and it is necessary to progress by metamorphoses of them."

Suddenly a naked man appears, seated in the middle of the sand with his legs crossed. A large circle vibrates, suspended behind him. The little curls of his black hair, deepening into an azure tint, twist symmetrically around a protuberance at the top of his head. His arms, of great length, fall straight down his sides. His two hands, with open palms, rest evenly on his thighs. The lower portions of his feet present the figures of two suns; and he remains completely motionless in front of Antony and Hilarion, with all the gods around him placed at intervals upon the rocks, as if on the seats of a circus. His lips open, and in a deep voice he says:

"I am the master of the great charity, the help of creatures, and I expound the law to believers and to the profane alike. To save the world I wished to be born amongst men; the gods wept when I went away. At first, I sought a woman suitable for the purpose—of warlike race, the spouse of a king, exceedingly virtuous and beautiful, with a deep navel, a body firm as a diamond; and at the time of the full moon, without the intervention of any male, I entered her womb. I came out through her right side. Then the stars stopped in their motions."

Hilarion murmurs between his teeth:

"'And when they saw the stars stop, they conceived a great joy!'"

Antony looks more attentively at the Buddha, who resumes:

"From the bottom of the Himalaya, a religious centenarian set forth to see me."

Hilarion—"'A man called Simeon, who was not to die before he had seen the Christ!'"

The Buddha—"They brought me to the schools. I knew more than the doctors."

Hilarion—" ... 'In the midst of the doctors; and all those who heard him were ravished by his wisdom.'"

Antony makes a sign to Hilarion to keep silent.

The Buddha—"I went continually to meditate in the gardens. The shadows of the trees used to move; but the shadow of the one that sheltered me did not move. No one could equal me in the knowledge of the Sacred Writings, the enumeration of atoms, the management of elephants, waxworks, astronomy, poetry, boxing, all exercises and all arts. In compliance with custom, I took a wife; and I passed the days in my royal palace, arrayed in pearls, under a shower of perfumes, fanned by the fly-flappers of thirty-three thousand women, and gazing at my people from the tops of my terraces adorned with resounding bells. But the sight of the world's miseries made me turn aside from pleasures. I fled. I went a-begging on high-ways, covered with rags collected in the sepulchres; and, as there was a very learned hermit, I offered myself as his servant. I guarded his door; I washed his feet. All sensation, all joy, all languor, were annihilated. Then, concentrating my thoughts on a larger field of meditation, I came to know the essence of things, the illusion of forms. I speedily abandoned the science of the Brakhmans. They are eaten up with lusts beneath their austere exterior; they anoint themselves with filth, and sleep upon thorns, believing that they arrive at happiness through the path of death!"

Hilarion—"Pharisees, hypocrites, whited sepulchres, race of vipers!"

The Buddha—"I, too, have done astonishing things—eating for a day only a single grain of rice—and at that time grains of rice were not bigger than they are now—my hair fell off; my body became black; my eyes, sunken in their sockets, seemed like stars seen at the bottom of a well. For six years I never moved, remaining exposed to flies, to lions, and to serpents; and I subjected myself to burning suns, heavy showers, snow, lightning, hail, and tempest, without even shielding myself with my hand. The travellers who passed, assuming that I was dead, flung clods of earth at me from a distance.

"There only remained for me to be tempted by the Devil.

"I invoked him.

"His sons came—hideous, covered with scales, nauseous as charcoal, howling, hissing, bellowing, flinging at each other armour and dead men's bones. Some of them spirted out flames through their nostrils; others spread around darkness with their wings; others carried chaplets of fingers that had been cut off; others drank the venom of serpents out of the hollows of their hands. They have the heads of pigs, rhinoceroses, or toads—all kinds of figures calculated to inspire respect or terror."

Antony, aside—"I endured that myself in former times."

The Buddha—"Then he sent me his daughters—beautiful, well-attired with golden girdles, teeth white as the jasmine, and limbs round as an elephant's trunk. Some of them stretched up their arms when they yawned to display the dimples in their elbows; others blinked their eyes; others began to laugh and others unfastened one another's garments. Amongst them were blushing virgins, matrons full of pride, and queens with great trains of baggage and attendants."

Antony, aside—"Ah! that also!"

The Buddha—"Having vanquished the demon. I passed twelve

years in nourishing myself exclusively on perfumes,—and, as I had acquired the five virtues, the five faculties, the ten forces, the eighteen substances and penetrated into the four spheres of the invisible world, the Intelligence was mine, and I became the Buddha!"

All the gods bow down, those who have many heads lower them all at the same time. He raises his hand on high in the air, and resumes:

"In view of the deliverance of beings, I have made hundreds of thousands of sacrifices; I have given to the poor robes of silk, beds, chariots, houses, heaps of gold and diamonds. I have given my hands to the one-handed, my legs to the lame, my eyes to the blind; I have cut off my head for the decapitated. At the time when I was king, I distributed the provinces; at the time when I was Brakhman, I despised nobody. When I was a solitary I spoke words of tenderness to the thief who tried to cut my throat. When I was a tiger, I let myself die of hunger. And in this final stage of existence, having preached the law, I have nothing more to do. The great period is accomplished. The men, the animals, the gods, the bamboos, the oceans, the mountains, the grains of sand of the Ganges, with the myriads of myriads of stars, everything, must perish; and, until the new births, a flame will dance on the ruins of a world's overthrow."

Then a vertigo seizes the gods. They stagger, fall into convulsions, and vomit forth their existences. Their crowns break to pieces; their standards fly away. They get rid of their attributes and their sexes, fling over their shoulders the cups from which they drink immortality, strangle themselves with their serpents, and vanish in smoke; and, when they have all disappeared:

Hilarion, slowly—"You have just seen the creed of many hundreds of millions of men!"

Antony is on the earth, his face in his hands. Standing close to him, and turning his back to the cross, Hilarion watches him.

A rather lengthened period elapses.

Then a singular being appears, with the head of a man and the body of a fish. He advances straight through the air, tossing the sand with his tail; and his patriarchal face and his little arms make Antony laugh.

Oannes, in a plaintive voice—"Treat me with respect! I am the contemporary of the beginning of things.

"I have dwelt in the shapeless world, where slumbered hermaphrodite animals, under the weight of an opaque atmosphere, in the depths of gloomy waves—when the fingers, the fins, and the wings were confounded, and eyes without heads floated like molluscs amongst human-faced bulls and dog-footed serpents.

"Over the whole of those beings Omoroca, bent like a hoop, stretched her woman's body. But Belus cut her clean in two halves, made the earth with one, and the heavens with another; and the two worlds alike mutually contemplate each other. I, the first consciousness of chaos, I have arisen from the abyss to harden matter, to regulate forms; and I have taught men fishing, the sowing of seed, the scripture, and the history of the gods. Since then, I live in the ponds that remained after the Deluge. But the desert grows larger around them; the wind flings sand into them; the sun consumes them; and I expire on my bed of lemon while gazing across the water at the stars. Thither am I returning."

He makes a plunge and disappears in the Nile.

Hilarion—"This is an ancient god of the Chaldeans!"

Antony, ironically—"Who, then, were the gods of Babylon?"

Hilarion—"You can see them!"

And they find themselves upon the platform of a quadrangular tower rising above other towers, which, growing narrower in

96

proportion as they rise, form a monstrous pyramid. You may distinguish below a great, black mass—the city, without doubt—stretching along the plain. The air is cold; the sky is of a sombre blue; the multitudinous stars palpitate.

In the middle of the platform stands a column of white stone. Priests in linen robes pass and return all round, so as to describe in their evolutions a moving circle, and, with heads raised, they contemplate the stars.

Hilarion points out several of them to Saint Antony:

"There are thirty chief priests. Fifteen gaze upon the region above the earth, and fifteen on the region below it. At regular intervals one of them rushes from the upper regions to the lower, whilst another abandons the lower to mount towards the empyrean.

"Of the seven planets, two are benevolent, two malevolent, and three ambiguous; everything in the world depends on these eternal fires. According to their position and their movements, one may draw prognostications, and you are now treading on the most sacred spot on earth. There Pythagoras and Zoroaster may be met. Two thousand years have these men been observing the sky, the better to comprehend the gods."

Antony—"The stars are not gods!"

Hilarion—"Yes! say they; for, while things are continually passing around us, the sky, like eternity, remains unchangeable!"

Antony—"Nevertheless, it has a master."

Hilarion, pointing at the column—"That is Belus, the first ray, the sun, the male!—the other, which is fruitful, is under him!"

Antony observes a garden lighted up with lamps. He is in the midst of the crowd in an avenue of cypress-trees. To right and left little paths lead towards huts erected in a wood of pomegranate-trees, which protect lattices of reeds. The men, for the most part, have pointed caps with laced robes, like the plumage of peacocks. There are people from the North clad in bearskins; nomads in brown woollen cloaks; pale Gangarides with long ear-rings; and the classes, like the nationalities, appear to be confused, for sailors and stone-cutters jostle against princes wearing tiaras of carbuncles and carrying large walking-sticks with carved heads. All hurry forward with dilated nostrils, filled with the same desire.

From time to time they got out of the way, in order to allow a long, covered chariot, drawn by oxen, to pass, or perhaps it is an ass jolting on his back a woman closely veiled, who also disappears in the direction of the huts.

Antony is frightened. He desires to turn back. However, an inexpressible curiosity leads him on.

Beneath the cypress-trees women are squatted in rows upon deerskins, each of them having for a diadem a plait of cords. Some of them, magnificently attired, address the passers-by in loud tones. The more timid keep their features hidden between their hands, whilst, from behind, a matron—no doubt, their mother—encourages them. Others, with heads enveloped in black shawls, and the rest of their bodies quite nude, seem, at a distance, like statues of flesh. As soon as a man flings money on their knees, they rise. And one can hear kisses amid the foliage, and sometimes a great, bitter cry.

Hilarion—"Those are the virgins of Babylon who prostitute themselves to the goddess."

Antony—"What goddess?"

Hilarion—"There she is!"

And he shows Antony, at the very end of the avenue, on the threshold of an illuminated grotto, a block of stone representing a woman.

Antony—"Infamy! What an abomination to give a sex to God!"

Hilarion—"You conceive Him, surely, as a living person!"

Once more Antony finds himself in darkness.

He perceives in the air a luminous circle placed on horizontal wings. This species of ring surrounds, like a girdle that is too loose, the figure of a small man with a mitre on his head and a crown in his hand, the lower part of whose body is shut out from view by the huge feathers exhibited in his kilt.

This is Ormuz, the God of the Persians. He flutters while he exclaims:

"I am terrified! I catch a glimpse of his mouth. I have vanquished thee, Ahriman! But thou art beginning again!

"At first, revolting against me, thou didst destroy the eldest of creatures, Kaiomortz, the man-bull. Then, thou didst seduce the first human pair, Meschia and Meschiana, and didst fill their hearts with darkness, and press forward thy battalions towards Heaven.

"I had my own, the inhabitants of the stars, and I gazed down from my throne on all the planets in their different spheres.

"Mithra, my son, dwelt in an inaccessible spot. There he received souls, and sent them forth, and, each morning he arose to pour out his riches.

"The splendour of the firmament was reflected by the earth. The fire shone on the mountains—image of the other fire with which I have created all beings. To secure it from defilement, they did not burn the dead, who were transported to Heaven on the beaks of birds.

"I have regulated pasturages, labours, the wood of sacrifice, the forms of cups, the words that must be uttered in insomnia; and my priests prayed continually in order that their worship should correspond to the eternity of God. They purified themselves with water; they offered up loaves on the altars; they confessed their sins in loud tones.

"Homa gave himself to men to drink in order to communicate his strength to them.

"While the genii of Heaven were fighting the demons, the children of Iran chased the serpents. The King, whom a countless train of courtiers served on bended knees, was attired so as to resemble me in person, and wore my head-dress. His gardens had the magnificence of a celestial earth; and his tomb represented him slaying a monster—emblem of the good which exterminates evil. For, one day, it came to pass—thanks to the endless course of time—that I triumphed over Ahriman. But the interval that separates us is disappearing; the night is rising! Help, Amschaspands, Irzeds, Ferouers! Come to my assistance, Mithra! take thy sword! Caosyac, who must come back to save the world, defend me! How is this? ... No one!

"Ah! I am dying! Ahriman, thou art the master!"

Hilarion, behind Antony, restrains an exclamation of joy, and Ormuz plunges into the darkness.

Then appears the great Diana of Ephesus, black, with enamelled eyes, elbows at her sides, forearms turned out, and hands open.

Lions crouch upon her shoulders; fruits, flowers and stars cross one another upon her chest; further down three rows of breasts exhibit themselves, and from the belly to the feet she is caught in a close sheath, from which sprout forth, in the centre of her body, bulls, stags, griffins and bees. She is seen in the white gleaming caused by a disc of silver, round as the full moon, placed behind her head.

"Where is my temple? Where are my amazons? How is it with me— me, the incorruptible—that I find myself so impotent?"

Her flowers wither; her fruits, over-ripe, hang loose; the lions and the bulls bow down their necks; the stags, exhausted, begin to pant; the bees, with a faint buzzing, fall dying upon the ground. She presses her breasts one after the other. They are empty! But, yielding to a desperate pressure, her sheath bursts open. She clutches the end of it, like the skirt of a dress, flings into it her animals and her flower-wreaths, then goes back into the darkness; and in the distance voices murmur, grumble, roar, cry, or bellow. The density of the night is increased by the winds. A warm shower begins to fall in heavy drops.

Antony—"How pleasant is this odour of palm-trees, this rustling of green leaves, this transparency of fountains! I would like to lie down flat upon the ground, in order to feel it close to my heart, and my life would be renewed in eternal youth!"

He hears the sound of castanets and cymbals, and, in the midst of a rustic crowd, men clad in white tunics, with red bands, lead out an ass, richly harnessed, his tail adorned with ribands and his hoofs painted. A box, covered with a saddle-cloth of yellow linen, sways to and fro upon his back, between two baskets, one of which receives the offerings deposited there—eggs, grapes, pears, cheeses, poultry, and small coins—while the second is full of roses, which the drivers of the ass scatter before him as they move along. The latter wear pendants in their ears, large cloaks, plaited tresses, and have their cheeks painted. Each of them has an olive crown fastened around his forehead by a figured medallion. They carry daggers in their girdles, and flourish whips with ebony handles, each having three thongs mounted with ossicles. The last in the procession fix in the ground erect, as a chandelier, a huge pine-tree, whose summit is on fire, and the lowest branches of which overshadow a little sheep.

The ass stops. The saddle-cloth is removed; and underneath appears a second covering of black felt. Then one of the men in a white tunic begins to dance, while playing upon castanets; while another, on his knees before the box, beats a tambourine; and the oldest of the band commences:

"Here is the Bona Dea, the divinity of the mountains, the great mother of Syria! Draw hither, honest people! She procures joy, heals the sick, bestows fortunes, and satisfies lovers. It is we who bring her out to walk in the country in fine weather and bad weather. We often sleep in the open air, and we have not a well-served table every day. The thieves dwell in the woods. The beasts rush forth from their dens. Slippery paths line the precipices. Look here! look here!"

They raise the coverlet and disclose a box incrusted with little pebbles.

"Higher than the cedar-trees she hovers in the blue ether. More circumambient than the winds, she surrounds the world. Her respiration is exhaled through the nostrils of tigers; her voice growls beneath the volcanoes; her anger is the storm; and the pallor of her face has made the moon white. She ripens the harvests; she swells out the rinds; she makes the beard grow. Give her something, for she hates the avaricious!"

The box flies open; and beneath an awning of blue silk is seen a little image of Cybele, glittering with spangles, crowned with towers, and seated on a chariot of red stone, drawn by two lions with raised paws.

The crowd presses forward to see.

The archi-gallus continues:

"She loves the sounds of dulcimers, the stamping of feet, the howling of wolves, the echoing mountains and the deep gorges, the flower of the almond-tree, the pomegranate and the green figs, the whirling dance, the high-sounding flute, the sweet sap, the salt tear,—blood! Help! help! Mother of mountains!"

They flagellate themselves with their whips, and the strokes resound on their breasts. The skins of the tambourines vibrate till they almost burst. They seize their knives and inflict gashes on their arms:

"She is sad: let us be sad! He who is doomed to suffer must weep! In that way your sins will be remitted. Blood washes out everything: shed drops of it around, then, like flowers. She demands that of another—of one who is pure!"

The archi-gallus raises his knife above the sheep,

Antony, seized with horror—"Don't slaughter the lamb!"

A purple flood gushes forth. The priests sprinkle the crowd with it; and all—including Antony and Hilarion—ranged around the burning tree, silently watch the last palpitations of the victim. From the midst of the priests comes a woman, exactly like the image enclosed in the little box. She stops on seeing a young man in a Phrygian cap.

His thighs are covered with tight-fitting breeches opened here and there by lozenges which are fastened with coloured bows. He rests his elbows against one of the branches of the tree, holding a flute in his hand, in a languishing attitude.

Cybele, encircling his figure with her arms—

"To rejoin thee I have travelled through every region—and famine ravaged the fields. Thou hast deceived me! No matter,—I love thee! Warm my body! Let us unite!"

Atys—"The spring-time will return no more, O eternal Mother! Despite my love, it is not possible to penetrate thy essence. I should like to cover myself with a coloured robe like thine. I envy thy breasts, swollen with milk, the length of thy tresses, thy mighty sides from which spring living creatures. Would that I were like thee! Would that I were woman! But no! that can never be! My virility fills me with horror!"

With a sharp stone he mutilates himself; then he begins to run madly around.

The priests imitate the god; the faithful, the priests. Men and women exchange their garments and embrace one another; and this whirlwind of blood-stained flesh hurries away, whilst the voices, ever continuing, become more clamorous and shrill, like those one hears at funerals.

A great catafalque hung with purple carries on its summit a bed of ebony, surrounded by torches and baskets of silver filigree, in which are contained green lettuces, mallows, and fennel. Upon the seats, above and below, are seated women, all attired in black, with girdles undone and naked feet, and holding with a melancholy air huge bouquets of flowers.

On the ground, at the corners of the platform, alabaster urns filled with myrrh are sending up light wreaths of smoke. On the bed may be seen the corpse of a man. Blood trickles from his thigh. His arm is hanging down, and a dog, who is howling, licks his nails. The line of torches placed too close to one another prevents his figure from being completely visible. Antony is seized with anguish. He is afraid of seeing the face of some one he knew.

The women cease their sobbing; and, after an interval of silence, all, at the same time, burst into a psalm:

"Beautiful! beautiful! he is beautiful! Enough of sleep—raise his head! Up! Inhale our bouquets! These are narcissi and anemones gathered in thy gardens to please thee. Return to life! thou fillest us with fear!

"Speak! What dost thou require? Dost thou wish to drink wine? Dost thou wish to sleep in our beds? Dost thou wish to eat the honey-cakes which have the form of little birds?

"Let us press close to his hips! let us kiss his breast! Hold! hold! feel thou our fingers covered with rings which are stealing over thy body, and our lips which are seeking thy mouth, and our hair which is sweeping thy legs, insensible god, deaf to our prayers!"

They burst into shrieks, tearing their faces with their nails, then become silent; and only the howling of the dog is heard.

104

"Alas! alas! The dark blood rushes over his snowy flesh. See how his knees writhe, how his sides give way! The flowers upon his face have soaked the gore. He is dead! Let us weep! let us lament!"

They come all in a row to fling down between the torches their flowing locks, resembling at a distance black or yellow serpents; and the catafalque is softly lowered to the level of a cave—a gloomy sepulchre, which is yawning in the background.

Then a woman bends over the corpse. Her hair, which never has been cut, covers her from head to foot. She sheds so many tears that her grief does not seem to be like that of others, but superhuman, infinite.

Antony thinks of the mother of Jesus.

She says:

"Thou didst escape from the East, and thou didst press me in thy arms all quivering with dew, O sun! Doves fluttered above the azure of thy mantle, our kisses caused breezes amid the foliage, and I abandoned myself to thy love, delighting in the exquisite sensation of my own weakness.

"Alas! alas! Why art thou about to rush away over the mountains? At the autumnal equinox a wild boar wounded thee! Thou art dead, and the fountains weep and the trees droop, and the winter wind is whistling through the leafless branches.

"My eyes are about to close, seeing that darkness is covering thee. By this time thou art dwelling on the other side of the world, near my more powerful rival.

"O Persephone, all that is beautiful goes down to thee and returns no more!"

While she has been speaking, her companions have taken the dead body to lower it into the sepulchre. It remains in their hands. It was only a corpse of wax!

Antony experiences a kind of relief. The whole scene vanishes, and the cell, the rocks, and the cross reappear! And now he distinguishes on the other side of the Nile a woman standing in the middle of the desert. She holds with her hand the end of a long black veil, which conceals her figure; while she carries on her left arm a little child, which she is suckling. At her side a huge ape is squatted on the sand. She lifts her head towards the sky, and, in spite of the distance, her voice can be heard.

Isis—"O Neith, beginning of things! Ammon, lord of eternity! Ptha, demiurgus! Thoth, his intelligence! Gods of Amenthi! Special Triads of the Nomes! Sparrow-hawks in the azure! Sphinxes on the outsides of temples! Ibises standing between the horns of oxen! Planets! Constellations! River-banks! Murmurs of wind! Reflections of light! Tell me where to find Osiris!

"I have sought for him through all the water-courses and all the lakes, and, farther still, in the Ph[oe]nician Byblos. Anubis, with ears erect, jumped round me, barking, and with his nose scenting out the clumps of tamarind. Thanks, good Cynocephalus, thanks!"

She gives the ape two or three friendly little slaps on the head.

"The hideous red-haired Typhon killed him and tore him to pieces. We have found all his members. But I have not got that which made me fruitful!"

She utters bitter lamentations.

Antony is seized with rage. He casts pebbles at her insultingly:

"Impure one! begone, begone!"

Hilarion—"Respect her! This is the religion of your ancestors! You have worn her amulets in your cradle!"

Isis—"In former times, when the summer returned, the inundation drove to the desert the impure beasts. The dykes flew open; the boats dashed against one another; the panting earth drank the

106

stream till it was glutted. O god! with horns of bull, thou didst stretch thyself upon my breast, and the lowing of the eternal cow was heard!

"The new-sown crops, the harvests, the thrashing of corn, and the vintages succeeded each other regularly in unison with the changes of the seasons. In the nights, ever clear, the great stars shed forth their beams. The days were steeped in an unchanging splendour. The sun and the moon were seen like a royal pair on either side of the horizon.

"We were enthroned in a world more sublime—twin monarchs, spouses from the bosom of eternity; he holding a sceptre with the head of a conchoupha, and I a sceptre with a lotus-flower, we stood with hands joined;—and the crash of empires did not change our attitude.

"Egypt lay stretched beneath us, monumental and solemn, long, like the corridor of a temple, with obelisks at the right, pyramids at the left, its labyrinth in the middle; and everywhere avenues of monsters, forests of columns, massive archways flanking gates which have for their summit the earth's sphere between two wings.

"The animals of her zodiac found their counterparts in her plains, and with their forms and colours filled her mysterious writings. Divided into twelve regions, as the year is into twelve months— each month, each day, having its god—she reproduced the immutable order of the heavens; and man, though he died, did not lose his lineaments, but, saturated with perfumes and becoming imperishable, he went to sleep for three thousand years in a silent Egypt.

"The latter, greater than the other, spread out beneath the earth. Thither one descended by means of staircases leading to halls where were reproduced the joys of the good, the tortures of the wicked, everything that takes place in the third invisible world. Ranged along the walls, the dead, in painted coffins, awaited each their turn; and the soul, free from migrations, continued its sleep till it awakened in another life.

"Meanwhile, Osiris sometimes came back to see me. His shade made me the mother of Harpocrates."

She gazes on the child:

"It is he! Those are his eyes; those are his tresses, curling like a ram's horns. Thou shalt begin his works over again. We shall bloom afresh, like the lotus. I am always the great Isis! Nobody has ever yet lifted my veil! My offspring is the sun!

"Sun of spring, let the clouds obscure thy face! The breath of Typhon devours the pyramids. Just now I have seen the Sphinx fly away. He galloped off like a jackal.

"I am seeking for my priests—my priests in their linen robes, with great harps, carrying along a mystic skiff ornamented with pateræ of silver. No more feasts on the lakes! no more illuminations in my Delta! no more cups of milk at Philæ! For a long time Apis has not reappeared.

"Egypt! Egypt! Thy great immovable gods have their shoulders whitened by the dung of birds, and the wind, as it passes along the desert, carries with it the ashes of the dead!—Anubis, protector of shadows, do not leave me!"

The Cynocephalus vanishes.

She gives her child a shaking.

"But what aileth thee? ... thy hands are cold, thy head fallen back!"

Harpocrates has just died. Then she utters a cry so bitter, mournful, and heartrending, that Antony replies to it by another cry, while he opens his arms to support her.

She is no longer there. He hangs his head, overwhelmed with shame.

All that he has just seen becomes confused in his mind. It is like the stunning effect of a voyage, the uncomfortable sensation of drunkenness. Fain would he hate; and yet a vague pity softens his heart. He begins to weep abundantly.

Hilarion—"What is it now that makes you sad?"

Antony, after questioning himself for a long time—"I am thinking of all the souls lost through these false gods!"

Hilarion—"Do you not find that they have—in some respects—resemblances to the true?"

Antony—"This is a trick of the Devil the better to seduce the faithful. He attacks the strong through the spirit, and the others through the flesh."

Hilarion—"But lust, in its furies, possesses the disinterestedness of penitence. The frantic love of the body accelerates its destruction—and by its weakness proclaims the extent of the impossible."

Antony—"How is it that this affects me? My heart revolts with disgust against those brutish gods, always occupied with carnage and incest."

Hilarion—"Recall to yourself in the Scriptures all the things that scandalise you because you cannot understand them. In the same way, these gods, under the outward form of criminals, may contain the truth. There are some of them left to see. Turn aside!"

Antony—"No! no! it is a peril!"

Hilarion—"A moment ago you wished to make their acquaintance. Do falsehoods make your faith totter? What do you fear?"

The rocks in front of Antony have become a mountain.

A range of clouds intersects it half-way from the top; and overhead appears another mountain, enormous, quite green, which hollows out the valley unevenly, having on its summit, in a wood of laurels, a palace of bronze, with tiles of gold and ivory capitals.

109

In the midst of the peristyle, upon a throne, Jupiter, colossal, and with a naked torso, holds victory in one hand, and the thunderbolt in the other; and his eagle, between his legs, erects its head.

Juno, close to him, rolls her great eyes, surmounted by a diadem, from which escapes, like a vapour, a veil floating in the wind.

Behind, Minerva, standing on a pedestal, leans upon her spear. The Gorgon's skin covers her breast, and a linen peplum descends in regular folds even to her toe-nails. Her grey eyes, which shine beneath her vizor, gaze intently into the distance.

At the right of the palace the aged Neptune is riding on a dolphin beating with its fins a vast expanse of azure, which is the sky or the sea, for the perspective of the ocean prolongs the blue ether; the two elements become mingled in one.

On the other side, Pluto, fierce, in a mantle black as night, with a tiara of diamonds and a sceptre of ebony, is in the midst of an isle enclosed by the windings of the Styx;—and this ghostly stream rushes into the darkness, which forms under the cliff a great black gap, a shapeless abyss.

Mars, clad in bronze, brandishes, with an air of fury, his huge sword and shield.

Hercules, standing lower, gazes up at him, leaning on his club.

Apollo, with radiant face, is driving, with his right arm extended, four white horses at a gallop; and Ceres, in a chariot drawn by oxen, is advancing towards him with a sickle in her hand.

Bacchus goes before her on a very low car slowly drawn along by lynxes. Erect, beardless, with vine-branches over his forehead, he passes, holding a goblet from which wine is flowing. Silenus, at his side, is dangling upon an ass. Pan, with pointed ears, is blowing his pipe; the Mimallones beat drums; Mænads scatter flowers; the Bacchantes throw back their heads with hair dishevelled.

Diana, with her tunic tucked up, sets out from the wood with her nymphs.

At the bottom of a cavern, Vulcan is hammering the iron between the Cabiri; here and there, the old river-gods, resting upon green stones, water their urns; and the Muses, standing up, are singing in the dales.

The Hours, of equal height, hold each other by the hand; and Mercury is placed in a slanting posture, upon a rainbow, with his magic wand, his winged sandals and his broad-brimmed hat.

But at the top of the staircase of the gods, amid clouds soft as feathers, whose folds as they wind around let fall roses, Venus Anadyomene is gazing at her image in a mirror; her pupils cast languishing glances underneath her rather heavy eyelashes. She has long, fair tresses, which spread out over her shoulders, her dainty breasts, her slender figure, her hips widening like the curves of a lyre, her two rounded thighs, the dimples around her knees, and her delicate feet. Not far from her mouth a butterfly is fluttering. The splendour of her body sheds around her a halo of brilliant mother-of-pearl; and all the rest of Olympus is bathed in a rosy dawn, which, by insensible degrees, reaches the heights of the azure sky.

Antony—"Ah! my bosom dilates. A joy, which I cannot analyse, descends into the depths of my soul. How beautiful it is! how beautiful it is!"

Hilarion—"They stooped down from the height of the clouds to direct the swords. You might meet them on the roadsides. You kept them in your home; and this familiarity made life divine.

"Her only aim was to be free and beautiful. Her ample robes rendered her movements more graceful. The orator's voice, exercised beside the sea, struck the marble porticoes in unison with the sonorous waves. The stripling, rubbed with oil, wrestled, quite naked, in the full light of day. The most religious action was to expose pure forms.

"Those men, too, respected spouses, the aged and suppliants. Behind the Temple of Hercules, an altar was raised to Pity.

"They used to immolate victims with flowers around their fingers. Memory was not even troubled by the decay of the dead, for there remained of them only a handful of ashes. The soul, mingled with the boundless ether, ascended to the gods!"

Bending towards Antony's ear:

"And they live for ever! The Emperor Constantine adores Apollo. You will find the Trinity in the mysteries of Samothrace, baptism in the case of Isis, the redemption in that of Mithra, the martyrdom of a god in the feasts of Bacchus. Proserpine is the Virgin; Aristæus, Jesus!"

Antony keeps his eyes cast down; then all at once he repeats the creed of Jerusalem—as he recollects it—emitting, after each phrase, a long sigh:

"'I believe in one only God, the Father;—and in one only Lord, Jesus Christ, first-born son of God, who became incarnate and was made man; who was crucified and buried; who ascended into Heaven; who will come to judge the living and the dead; whose kingdom will have no end;—and in one only Holy Ghost;—and in one only baptism of repentance;—and in one holy Catholic Church;—and in the resurrection of the flesh;—and in the life everlasting!'"

Immediately the cross becomes larger, and, piercing the clouds, it casts a shadow over the heaven of the gods.

They all grow dim. Olympus vanishes.

Antony distinguishes near its base, half lost in the caverns, or supporting the stones on their shoulders, huge bodies chained.

These are the Titans, the Giants, the Hecatonchires, and the Cyclops.

A voice rises, indistinct and formidable,—like the murmur of the waves, like the sound heard in woods during a storm, like the roaring of the wind down a precipice:

"We knew it, we of all others! The gods were doomed to die. Uranus was mutilated by Saturn, and Saturn by Jupiter. He will be himself annihilated. Each in its turn. It is destiny!"

And, by degrees, they plunge into the mountain, and disappear.

Meanwhile, the roof of the palace of gold flies away.

Jupiter descends from his throne. The thunder at his feet smokes like a brand that is almost extinguished; and the eagle, stretching its neck, gathers with its beak its falling plumes.

"So, then, I am no longer the master of things, all-good, all-powerful, god of the phratriæ and of the Greek peoples, ancestor of all the kings, the Agamemnon of Heaven!

"Eagle of the apotheoses, what breath of Erebus has driven thee to me? or, flying from the Campus Martius, dost thou bring to me the soul of the last of the Emperors?

"I no longer desire those of men! Let the earth guard them, and let them be moved on a level with its baseness. They now have hearts of slaves; they forget injuries, ancestors, oaths; and everywhere the folly of mobs, the mediocrity of the individual, and the hideousness of races reign supreme!"

His respiration makes his sides swell even to bursting, and he writhes with his hands. Hebe in tears presents a cup to him. He seizes it:

"No! no! As long as there will be, no matter where, a head enclosing thought which hates disorder and realises the idea of Law, the spirit of Jupiter will live!"

But the cup is empty. He turns it around slowly on his finger-nail.

"Not a drop! When ambrosia fails, there is an end of the Immortals!"

It slips out of his hand, and he leans against a pillar, feeling that he is dying.

Juno—"There was no need of so many loves! Eagle, bull, swan, golden shower, cloud and flame, thou hast assumed every form, scattered thy light in every element, hidden thy head on every couch! This time the divorce is irrevocable—and our sway, our very existence, is dissolved!"

She rushes away into the air!

Minerva no longer has her spear; and the ravens, which nestled in the sculptures of the frieze, whirl round her, and bite at her helmet.

"Let me see whether my vessels, cleaving the shining sea, have returned into my three ports, wherefore the fields are deserted, and what the daughters of Athens are now doing.

"In the month of Hecatombæon, all my people came to me led by their magistrates and priests. Then, in white robes, with chitons of gold, the long files of virgins advanced, holding cups, baskets, and parasols; then, the three hundred oxen for the sacrifice, old men shaking green boughs, soldiers clashing their armour against each other, youths singing hymns, players on the flute and on the lyre, rhapsodists and dancing-girls—and finally, on the mast of a trireme, supported by coils of rope, my great veil embroidered by virgins, who, for the space of a year, had been nourished in a particular fashion; and, when it had been shown in every street, in every square, and before every temple, in the midst of a procession continually chanting, it ascended to the Acropolis, brushed passed the Propylæum, and entered the Parthenon.

"But a difficulty faces me—me, the ingenious one! What! what! not a single idea! Here am I more terrified than a woman."

She perceives behind her a ruin, utters a cry, and, struck on the forehead, falls backward to the ground.

Hercules has cast off his lion's skin, and, resting on his feet, bending his back, and biting his lips, he makes desperate efforts to sustain Olympus, which is toppling down.

"I have vanquished the Cercopes, the Amazons, and the Centaurs. I have slain many kings, I have broken the horn of Achelous, a great river. I have cut through mountains; I have brought oceans together. I have liberated enslaved nations; I have peopled uninhabited countries. I have travelled over Gaul. I have traversed the desert where one feels thirst. I have defended the gods, and I have freed myself from Omphale. But Olympus is too heavy. My arms are growing feeble. I am dying!"

He is crushed beneath the ruins.

Pluto—"It is thine own fault, Amphitrionades! Why didst thou descend into my realms? The vulture who devours the entrails of Tityus has raised its head; Tantalus has had his lips moistened; and Ixion's wheel is stopped.

"Meanwhile, the Keres stretch forth their nails to detain the souls; the Furies in despair twist the serpents in their locks; and Cerberus, fastened by thee with a chain, has a rattling in the throat, while he slavers from his three mouths.

"Thou didst leave the gate ajar. Others have come. The light of human day has penetrated Tartarus!"

He sinks into the darkness.

Neptune—"My trident no longer raises tempests. The monsters who caused terror have rotted at the bottom of the sea.

"Amphitrite, whose white feet rushed over the foam; the green nereids, who could be seen on the horizon; the scaly sirens, who used to stop the ships to tell stories; and the old tritons, who used to blow into shells, all are dead! The gaiety of the sea has vanished!

"I will not survive it! Let the vast ocean cover me."

He disappears into the azure.

Diana, attired in black, among her dogs, who have become wolves—

"The freedom of great woods intoxicated me with its odour of deer and exhalations of swamps. The women, over whose pregnancy I watched, bring dead children into the world. The moon trembles under the incantations of sorcerers. I am filled with violent and boundless desires. I long to drink poisons, to lose myself in vapours or in dreams! ..."

And a passing cloud bears her away.

Mars, bare-headed and blood-stained—

"At first, I fought single-handed, provoking by insults an entire army, indifferent to countries, and for the pleasure of carnage. Then, I had companions. They marched to the sound of flutes, in good order, with even step, breathing upon their bucklers, with lofty plume and slanting spear. We flung ourselves into the battle with loud cries like those of eagles. War was as joyous as a feast. Three hundred men withstood all Asia.

"But they returned, those barbarians! and in tens of thousands, nay, in millions! Since numbers, war-engines, and strategy are more powerful, it is better to make an end of it, like a brave man!"

He kills himself.

Vulcan, wiping the sweat from his limbs with a sponge—

"The world is getting cold. It is necessary to heat the springs, the volcanoes, and the rivers, which run from metals under the earth!— Strike harder! with vigorous arm! with all your strength!"

The Cabiri hurt themselves with their hammers, blind themselves with the sparks, and, groping their way along, are lost in the shadow.

Ceres, standing in her chariot which is drawn by wheels having wings in their naves—"Stop! Stop!

"They had good reason to exclude the strangers, the atheists, the epicureans, and the Christians! The mystery of the basket is unveiled, the sanctuary profaned—all is lost!"

She descends with a rapid fall—bursting into exclamation of despair, and dragging back the horses.

"Ah! falsehood! Daira is not given up to me. The brazen bell calls me to the dead. It is another kind of Tartarus. There is no returning from it. Horror!"

The abyss swallows her up.

Bacchus, laughing frantically:

"What does it matter! The wife of Archontes is my spouse! Even the law goes down before drunkenness. For me the new song and the multiplied forms!

"The fire which consumed my mother runs in my veins. Let it burn the stronger, even though I perish!

"Male and female, good for both, I deliver myself to ye, Bacchantes! I deliver myself to ye, Bacchantes! and the vine will twist around the trunks of trees! Howl! dance! writhe! Unbind the tiger and the slave! bite the flesh with ferocious teeth!"

And Pan, Silenus, the Satyrs, the Bacchantes, the Mimallones, and the Mænades, with their serpents, their torches, and their black masks, scatter flowers, then shake their dulcimers, strike their thyrsi, pelt each other with shells, crunch grapes, strangle a he-goat, and rend Bacchus.

Apollo, lashing his coursers, whose glistening hairs fly off—

"I have left behind me Delos the stony, so empty that everything there now seems dead; and I am striving to reach the Delphian oracle before its inspiring vapour should be completely lost. The mules browse on its laurel. The pythoness, gone astray, is found there no longer.

"By a stronger concentration, I will have sublime poems, eternal monuments; and all matter will be penetrated with the vibrations of my cithara."

He fingers its chords. They break and snap against his face. He flings down the instrument, and driving his four-horse chariot furiously:

"No! enough of forms! Farther still—to the very summit—to the world of pure thought!"

But the horses, falling back, begin to prance so that the chariot is smashed; and, entangled in the fragments of the pole and the knottings of the horses, he falls head-foremost into the abyss.

The sky is darkened. Venus, blue as a violet from the cold, shivers.

"I covered with my girdle the entire horizon of Hellas. Its fields shone with the roses of my cheeks; its shores were cut according to the form of my lips; and its mountains, whiter than my doves, palpitated under the hands of the sculptors. My spirit showed itself in the order of festivities, the arrangements of head-dresses, the dialogues of philosophers, and the constitution of republics. But I have loved men too much. It is Love that has dishonoured me!"

She falls back in tears.

"The world is abominable. My bosom feels the lack of air.

"O Mercury, inventor of the lyre, and conductor of souls, bear me away!"

She places a finger upon her mouth, and, describing an immense parabola, topples over into the abyss.

And now nothing can be seen. The darkness is complete.

In the meantime two red arrows seem to escape from the pupils of Hilarion.

Antony at length notices his high stature:

"Many times already, while you were speaking, you appeared to me to be growing tall; and it was not an illusion. How is this? Explain it to me. Your appearance appals me!"

Steps draw nigh.

"What is this now?"

Hilarion stretches forth his arms:

"Look!"

Then, under a pale ray of the moon, Antony distinguishes an interminable caravan which defiles over the crest of the rocks; and each passenger, one after another, falls from the cliff into the gulf.

First, there are the three great gods of Samothrace—Axieros, Axiokeros, and Axiokersa—joined in a cluster, with purple masks, and their hands raised.

Æsculapius advances with a melancholy air, without even seeing Samos and Telesphorus, who question him with anguish. Sosipolis, the Elean, with the form of a python, rolls out his rings towards the abyss. Doesp[oe]na, through vertigo, flings herself in there of her own accord. Britomartis, shrieking with fear, clasps the folds of her fillet. The Centaurs arrive with a great galloping, and dash, pell-mell, into the black hole.

Limping behind them come the sad group of nymphs. Those of the meadows are covered with dust; those of the woods groan and bleed, wounded by the woodcutters' axes.

The Gelludæ, the Stryges, the Empusæ, all the infernal goddesses intermingling their hooks, their torches, and their snakes, form a pyramid; and at the summit, upon a vulture's skin, Eurynomus, bluish like flesh-flies, devours his own arms.

119

Then in a whirlwind disappears at the same time, Orthia the sanguinary, Hymnia of Orchomena, the Saphria of the Patræans, Aphia of Ægina, Bendis of Thrace, and Stymphalia with the leg of a bird. Triopas, in place of three eyeballs, has nothing more than three orbits. Erichthonius, with spindle-shanks, crawls like a cripple on his wrists.

Hilarion—"What happiness, is it not, to see all of them in a state of abjectness and agony? Mount with me on this stone, and you will be like Xerxes reviewing his army.

"Yonder, at a great distance, in the midst of fogs, do you perceive that giant with yellow beard who lets fall a sword red with blood? He is the Scythian Zalmoxis between two planets—Artimpasa, Venus; and Orsiloche, the Moon.

"Farther off, emerging out of the pale clouds, are the gods who are adored by the Cimmerians, beyond even Thule!

"Their great halls were warm, and by the light of the naked swords that covered the vault they drank hydromel in horns of ivory. They ate the liver of the whale in copper plates forged by the demons, or else they listened to the captive sorcerers sweeping their hands across the harps of stone. They are weary! they are cold! The snow wears down their bearskins, and their feet are exposed through the rents in their sandals.

"They mourn for the meadows where, upon hillocks of grass, they used to recover breath in the battle, the long ships whose prows cut through the mountains of ice, and the skates they used in order to follow the orbit of the poles while carrying on the extremities of their arms the firmament, which turned around with them."

A shower of hoar-frost pours down upon them. Antony lowers his glance to the opposite side, and he perceives—outlining themselves in black upon a red background—strange personages with chin-pieces and gauntlets, who throw balls at one another, leap one on top of the other, make grimaces, and dance frantically.

120

Hilarion—"These are the gods of Etruria, the innumerable Æsars. Here is Tages, the inventor of auguries. He attempts with one hand to increase the divisions of the heavens, while with the other he leans upon the earth. Let him come back to it!

"Nortia is contemplating the wall into which she drove nails to mark the number of the years. Its surface is covered and its last period accomplished. Like two travellers driven about by a tempest, Kastur and Polutuk take shelter under the same mantle."

Antony, closes his eyes—"Enough! Enough!"

But now through the air with a great noise of wings pass all the Victories of the Capitol, hiding their foreheads in their hands, and losing the trophies suspended from their arms.

Janus, master of the twilight, flies away upon a black ram, and of his two faces one is already putrefied, while the other is benumbed with fatigue.

Summanus—god of the gloomy sky, who no longer has a head—presses against his heart an old cake in the form of a wheel.

Vesta, under a ruined cupola, tries to rekindle her extinguished lamp.

Bellona gashes her cheeks without causing the blood, which used to purify her devotees, to flow out.

Antony—"Pardon! They weary me!"

Hilarion—"Formerly they used to be entertaining!"

And he points out to Antony, in a grove of beech-trees a woman perfectly naked—with four paws like a beast—bestridden by a black man holding in each hand a torch.

"This is the goddess Aricia with the demon Virbius. Her priest, the monarch of the woods, happened to be an assassin; and the fugitive slaves, the despoilers of corpses, the brigands of the Salarian road, the cripples of the Sublician bridge, all the vermin of the garrets of the Suburra, had not dearer devotion!

"The patrician ladies of Mark Antony's time preferred Libitina."

And he shows him under the cypresses and rose-trees another woman clothed in gauze. She smiles, though she is surrounded by pickaxes, litters, black hangings, and all the utensils of funerals. Her diamonds glitter from afar among cobwebs. The Larvæ, like skeletons, display their bones amid the branches, and the Lemures, who are phantoms, spread out their bats' wings.

On the side of a field the god Terma is bent down, torn asunder, and covered with filth.

In the midst of a ridge the huge corpse of Vertumnus is being devoured by red dogs. The rustic gods depart weeping, Sartor, Sarrator, Vervactor, Eollina, Vallona, and Hostilenus—all covered with little hooded cloaks, and each bearing a mattock, a fork, a hurdle, and a boar-spear.

Hilarion—"It was their spirits that made the villa prosper with its dove-cotes, its park for dormice, its poultry-yards protected by snares, and its hot stables embalmed with cedar.

"They protected all the wretched people who dragged the fetters with their legs over the pebbles of the Sabina, those who called the hogs with the sound of the trumpet, those who gathered the grapes on the tops of the elm-trees, those who drove through the by-roads the asses laden with dung. The husbandman, while he panted over the handle of his plough, prayed to them to strengthen his arms; and the cow-herds, in the shadow of the lime-trees, beside gourds of milk, chanted their eulogies by turns upon flutes of reeds."

Antony sighs.

And in the middle of a chamber, upon a platform, a bed of ivory is revealed, surrounded by persons lifting up pine-torches.

"Those are the gods of marriage. They are awaiting the bride.

"Domiduca has to lead her in, Virgo to undo her girdle, Subigo to stretch her upon the bed, and Præma to keep back her arms, whispering sweet words in her ear.

"But she will not come! and they dismiss the others—Nona and Decima, the nurses; the three Nixii, who are to deliver her; the two wet-nurses, Educa and Potina; and Carna, the cradle-rocker, whose bunch of hawthorns drives away bad dreams from the infant. Later, Ossipago will have strengthened its knees, Barbatus will have given the beard, Stimula the first desires, and Volupia the first enjoyment; Fabulinus will have taught it how to speak, Numera how to count, Cam[oe]na how to sing, and Consus how to think."

The chamber is empty, and there remains no longer at the side of the bed anyone but Nænia—a hundred years old—muttering to herself the lament which she poured forth on the death of old men.

But soon her voice is lost amid bitter cries, which come from the domestic lares, squatted at the end of the atrium, clad in dogs' skins, with flowers around their bodies, holding their closed hands up to their cheeks, and weeping as much as they can.

"Where is the portion of food which is given to us at each meal, the good attentions of maid-servant, the smile of the matron, and the gaiety of the little boys playing with huckle-bones on the mosaic of the courtyard? Then, when they have grown big, they hang over our breasts their gold or leather bullæ.

"What happiness, when, on the evening of a triumph, the master, returning home, turned towards us his humid eyes! He told the story of his contests, and the narrow house was more stately than a palace, and more sacred than a temple.

"How pleasant were the repasts of the family, especially the day after the Feralia! The feeling of tenderness towards the dead dispelled all discords; and people embraced one another, drinking to the glories of the past, and to the hopes of the future.

"But the ancestors in painted wax, shut up behind us, became gradually covered with mouldiness. The new races, to punish us for their own deceptions, have broken our jaws; and under the rats' teeth our bodies of wood have crumbled away."

And the innumerable gods, watching at the doors, in the kitchen, in the cellar, and in the stoves, disperse on all sides, under the appearance of enormous ants running away, or huge butterflies on the wing.

Then a thunderclap.

A voice—"I was the God of armies, the Lord, the Lord God!

"I have unfolded on the hills the tents of Jacob, and nourished in the sands my fugitive people. It was I who burned Sodom! It was I who engulfed the earth beneath the Deluge! It was I who drowned Pharaoh, with the royal princes, the war-chariots, and the charioteers. A jealous God, I execrated the other gods. I crushed the impure; I overthrew the proud; and my desolation rushed to right and left, like a dromedary let loose in a field of maize.

"To set Israel free, I chose the simple. Angels, with wings of flame, spoke to them in the bushes.

"Perfumed with spikenard, cinnamon, and myrrh, with transparent robes and high-heeled shoes, women of intrepid heart went forth to slay the captains. The passing wind bore away the prophets.

"I engraved my law on tablets of stone. It shut in my people as in a citadel. They were my people. I was their God! The earth was mine, and men were mine, with their thoughts, their works, the implements with which they tilled the soil, and their posterity.

"My ark rested in a triple sanctuary, behind purple curtains and flaming lamps. For my ministry I had an entire tribe, who swung the censers, and the high-priest in a robe of hyacinth, and wearing precious stones upon his breast arranged in regular order.

"Woe! woe! The Holy of Holies is flung open; the veil is rent; the odours of the holocaust are scattered to all the winds. The jackals whine in the sepulchres; my temple is destroyed; my people are dispersed!

"They have strangled the priests with the cords of their vestments. The women are captives; the sacred vessels are all melted down!"

The voice, dying away:

"I was the God of armies, the Lord, the Lord God!" Then comes an appalling silence, a profound darkness.

Antony—"They are all gone!"

"I remain!" says some one.

And, face to face with him stands Hilarion, but transfigured—beautiful as an archangel, luminous as a sun, and so tall that, in order to see him, Antony lifts up his head—"Who, then, are you?"

Hilarion—"My kingdom is as wide as the universe, and my desire has no limits. I am always going about enfranchising the mind and weighing the worlds, without hate, without fear, without love, and without God. I am called Science."

Antony, recoiling backwards—"You must be, rather, the Devil!"

Hilarion, fixing his eyes upon him—"Do you wish to see him?"

Antony no longer avoids his glance. He is seized with curiosity concerning the Devil. His terror increases; his longing becomes measureless.

"If I saw him, however—if I saw him?" ... Then, in a spasm of rage:

"The horror that I have of him will rid me of him forever. Yes!"

A cloven foot reveals itself. Antony is filled with regret. But the Devil overshadows him with his horns, and carries him off.

125

CHAPTER VI

The Mystery of Space

HE flies under Antony's body, extended like a swimmer; his two great wings, outspread, entirely concealing him, resemble a cloud.

Antony—"Where am I going? Just now I caught a glimpse of the form of the Accursèd One. No! a cloud is carrying me away. Perhaps I am dead, and am mounting up to God? ...

"Ah! how well I breathe! The untainted air inflates my soul. No more heaviness! no more suffering!

"Beneath me, the thunderbolt darts forth, the horizon widens, rivers cross one another. That light spot is the desert; that pool of water the ocean. And other oceans appear—immense regions of which I had no knowledge. There are black lands that smoke like live embers, a belt of snow ever obscured by the mists. I am trying to discover the mountains where each evening the sun goes to sleep."

The Devil—"The sun never goes to sleep!"

Antony is not startled by this voice. It appears to him an echo of his thought—a response of his memory.

Meanwhile, the earth takes the form of a ball, and he perceives it in the midst of the azure turning on its poles while it winds around the sun.

The Devil—"So, then, it is not the centre of the world? Pride of man, humble thyself!"

Antony—"I can scarcely distinguish it now. It is intermingled with the other fires. The firmament is but a tissue of stars."

They continue to ascend.

"No noise! not even the crying of the eagles! Nothing! ... and I bend down to listen to the music of the spheres."

The Devil—"You cannot hear them! No longer will you see the antichthon of Plato, the focus of Philolaüs, the spheres of Aristotle, or the seven heavens of the Jews with the great waters above the vault of crystal!"

Antony—"From below it appeared as solid as a wall. But now, on the contrary, I am penetrating it; I am plunging into it!"

And he arrives in front of the moon—which is like a piece of ice, quite round, filled with a motionless light.

The Devil—"This was formerly the abode of souls. The good Pythagoras had even supplied it with birds and magnificent flowers."

Antony—"I see nothing there save desolate plains, with extinct craters, under a black sky.

"Come towards those stars with a softer radiance, so that we may gaze upon the angels who hold them with the ends of their arms, like torches!"

The Devil carries him into the midst of the stars.

"They attract one another at the same time that they repel one another. The action of each has an effect on the others, and helps to produce their movements—and all this without the medium of an auxiliary, by the force of a law, by the virtue simply of order."

Antony—"Yes ... yes! my intelligence grasps it! It is a joy greater than the sweetness of affection! I pant with stupefaction before the immensity of God!"

The Devil—"Like the firmament, which rises in proportion as you ascend, He will become greater according as your imagination mounts higher; and you will feel your joy increase in proportion to the unfolding of the universe, in this enlargement of the Infinite."

Antony—"Ah! higher! ever higher!"

The stars multiply and shed around their scintillations. The Milky Way at the zenith spreads out like an immense belt, with gaps here and there; in these clefts, amid its brightness, dark tracts reveal themselves. There are showers of stars, trains of golden dust, luminous vapours which float and then dissolve.

Sometimes a comet sweeps by suddenly; then the tranquillity of the countless lights is renewed.

Antony, with open arms, leans on the Devil's two horns, thus occupying the entire space covered by his wings. He recalls with disdain the ignorance of former days, the limitation of his ideas. Here, then, close beside him, were those luminous globes which he used to gaze at from below. He traces the crossing of their paths, the complexity of their directions. He sees them coming from afar, and, suspended like stones in a sling, describing their orbits and pushing forward their parabolas.

He perceives, with a single glance, the Southern Cross and the Great Bear, the Lynx and the Centaur, the nebulæ of the Gold-fish, the six suns in the constellation of Orion, Jupiter with his four satellites, and the triple ring of the monstrous Saturn! all the planets, all the stars which men should, in future days, discover! He fills his eyes with their light; he overloads his mind with a calculation of their distances;—then he lets his head fall once more.

"What is the object of all this?"

The Devil—"There is no object!

"How could God have had an object? What experience could have enlightened Him, what reflection enabled Him to judge? Before the beginning of things, it would not have operated, and now it would be useless."

Antony—"Nevertheless, He created the world, at one period of time, by His mere word!"

The Devil—"But the beings who inhabit the earth came there successively. In the same way, in the sky, new stars arise—different effects from various causes."

Antony—"The variety of causes is the will of God!"

The Devil—"But to admit in God several acts of will is to admit several causes, and thus to destroy His unity!

"His will is not separable from His essence. He cannot have a second will, inasmuch as He cannot have a second essence—and, since He exists eternally, He acts eternally.

"Look at the sun! From its borders escape great flames emitting sparks which scatter themselves to become new worlds; and, further than the last, beyond those depths where only night is visible, other suns whirl round, and behind these others again, and others still, to infinity ..."

Antony—"Enough! enough! I am terrified! I am about to fall into the abyss."

The Devil stops, and gently balancing himself—

"There is no such thing as nothingness! There is no vacuum! Everywhere there are bodies moving over the unchangeable realms of space—and, as if it had any bounds it would not be space but a body, it consequently has no limits!"

Antony, open-mouthed—"No limits!"

The Devil—"Ascend into the sky forever and ever, and you will never reach the top! Descend beneath the earth for millions upon millions of centuries, and you will never get to the bottom—inasmuch as there is no bottom, no top, no end, above or below; and space is, in fact, comprised in God, who is not a part of space, of a magnitude that can be measured, but immensity!"

Antony, slowly—"Matter, in that case, would be part of God?"

129

The Devil—"Why not? Can you tell where He comes to an end?"

Antony—"On the contrary, I prostrate myself, I efface myself before His power!"

The Devil—"And you pretend to move Him! You speak to Him, you even adorn Him with virtues—goodness, justice, clemency,—in place of recognising the fact that He possesses all perfections!

"To conceive anything beyond is to conceive God outside of God. Being outside of Being. But then He is the only Being, the only Substance.

"If substance could be divided, it would lose its nature—it would not be itself; God would no longer exist. He is, therefore, indivisible as well as infinite, and if He had a body, He would be made up of parts. He would no longer be one; He would no longer be infinite. Therefore, He is not a person!"

Antony—"What? My prayers, my sobs, the sufferings of my flesh, the transports of my zeal, all these things would be no better than a lie ... in space ... uselessly—like a bird's cry, like a whirlwind of dead leaves!"

He weeps.

"Oh! no! There is above everything some One, a Great Spirit, a Lord, a Father, whom my heart adores, and who must love me!"

The Devil—"You desire that God should not be God; for, if He experienced love, anger, or pity, He would pass from His perfection to a greater or less perfection. He cannot descend to a sentiment, or be contained under a form."

Antony—"One day, however, I shall see Him!"

The Devil—"With the Blessèd, is it not? When the finite shall enjoy the Infinite, enclosing the Absolute in a limited space!"

Antony—"No matter! There must be a Paradise for the good, as well as a Hell for the wicked!"

The Devil—"Does the exigency of your reason constitute the law of things? Without doubt, evil is a matter of indifference to God, seeing that the earth is covered with it!

"Is it from impotence that He endures it, or from cruelty that He preserves it?

"Do you think that He can be continually putting the world in order like an imperfect work, and that He watches over all the movements of all beings, from the flight of the butterfly to the thought of man?

"If He created the universe His providence is superfluous. If Providence exists, creation is defective.

"But good and evil only concern you—like day and night, pleasure and pain, death and birth, which have relationship merely to a corner of space, to a special medium, to a particular interest. Inasmuch as what is infinite alone is permanent, the Infinite exists; and that is all!"

The Devil has gradually extended his huge wings, and now they cover space.

Antony can no longer see. He is on the point of fainting:

"A horrible chill freezes me to the bottom of my soul. This exceeds the utmost pitch of pain. It is, as it were, a death more profound than death. I wheel through the immensity of darkness. It enters into me. My consciousness is shivered to atoms under this expansion of nothingness."

The Devil—"But things happen only through the medium of your mind. Like a concave mirror, it distorts objects, and you need every resource in order to verify facts.

"Never shall you understand the universe in its full extent; consequently you cannot form an idea as to its cause, so as to have a just notion of God, or even say that the universe is infinite, for you should first comprehend the Infinite!

"Form is perhaps an error of your senses, substance an illusion of your intellect. Unless it be that the world, being a perpetual flux of things, appearances, by a sort of contradiction, would not be a test of truth, and illusion would be the only reality.

"But are you sure that you see? Are you sure that you live? Perhaps nothing at all exists!"

The Devil has seized Antony, and, holding him by the extremities of his arms, stares at him with open jaws ready to swallow him up.

"Come, adore me! and curse the phantom that you call God!"

Antony raises his eyes with a last movement of lingering hope.

The Devil quits him.

CHAPTER VII

The Chimera and the Sphinx

ANTONY finds himself stretched on his back at the edge of the cliff. The sky is beginning to grow white.

"Is this the brightness of dawn? or is it the reflection of the moon?" He tries to rise, then sinks back, and with chattering teeth:

"I feel fatigued ... as if all my bones were broken!

"Why?

"Ah! it is the Devil! I remember; and he even repeated to me all I had learned from old Didymus concerning the opinions of Xenophanes, of Heraclitus, of Melissus, and of Anaxagoras, as well as concerning the Infinite, the creation, and the impossibility of knowing anything!

"And I imagined that I could unite myself to God!"

Laughing bitterly:

"Ah! madness! madness! Is it my fault? Prayer is intolerable to me! My heart is drier than a rock! Formerly it overflowed with love! ...

"The sand, in the morning, used to send forth exhalations on the horizon, like the fumes of a censer. At the setting of the sun blossoms of fire burst forth from the cross, and, in the middle of the night, it often seemed to me that all creatures and all things, gathered in the same silence, were with me adoring the Lord. Oh! charm of prayer, bliss of ecstasy, gifts of Heaven, what has become of you?

"I remember a journey I made with Ammon in search of a solitude in which we might establish monasteries. It was the last evening, and we quickened our steps, murmuring hymns, side by side, without uttering a word. In proportion as the sun went down, the shadows of our bodies lengthened, like two obelisks, always enlarging and marching on in front of us. With the pieces of our staffs we planted the cross here and there to mark the site of a cell. The night came on slowly, and black waves spread over the earth, while an immense sheet of red still occupied the sky.

"When I was a child, I used to amuse myself in constructing hermitages with pebbles. My mother, close beside me, used to watch what I was doing.

"She was going to curse me for abandoning her, tearing her white locks. And her corpse remained stretched in the middle of the cell, beneath the roof of reeds, between the tottering walls. Through a hole, a hyena, sniffing, thrusts forward his jaws! ... Horror! horror!"

He sobs.

"No: Ammonaria would not have left her!

"Where is Ammonaria now?

"Perhaps, in a hot bath she is drawing off her garments one by one, first her cloak, then her girdle, then her outer tunic, then her inner one, then the wrappings round her neck; and the vapour of cinnamon envelops her naked limbs. At last she sinks to sleep on the tepid floor. Her hair, falling around her hips, looks like a black fleece—and, almost suffocating in the overheated atmosphere, she draws breath, with her body bent forward and her breasts projecting. Hold! here is my flesh breaking into revolt. In the midst of anguish, I am tortured by voluptuousness. Two punishments at the same time—it is too much! I can no longer endure my own body!"

He stoops down and gazes over the precipice.

"The man who falls over that will be killed. Nothing easier, by simply rolling over on the left side: it is necessary to take only one step! only one!"

Then appears an old woman.

Antony rises with a start of error. He imagines that he sees his mother risen from the dead.

But this one is much older and excessively emaciated. A winding-sheet, fastened round her head, hangs with her white hair down to the very extremities of her legs, thin as sticks. The brilliancy of her teeth, which are like ivory, makes her clayey skin look darker. The sockets of her eyes are full of gloom, and in their depths flicker two flames, like lamps in a sepulchre.

"Come forward," she says; "what keeps you back?"

Antony, stammering—"I am afraid of committing a sin!"

She resumes:

"But King Saul was slain! Razias, a just man, was slain! Saint Pelagius of Antioch was slain! Dominius of Aleppo and his two daughters, three more saints, were slain;—and recall to your mind all the confessors who, in their eagerness to die, rushed to meet their executioners. In order to taste death the more speedily, the virgins of Miletus strangled themselves with their cords. The philosopher, Hegesias, at Syracuse preached so well on the subject, that people deserted the brothels to hang themselves in the fields. The Roman patricians sought for death as if it were a debauch."

Antony—"Yes, it is a powerful passion! Many an anchorite has yielded to it."

The old woman—"To do a thing which makes you equal to God—think of that! He created you; you are about to destroy His work, you, by your courage, freely. The enjoyment of Erostrates was not greater. And then, your body is thus mocked by your soul in order that you may avenge yourself in the end. You will have no pain. It

135

will soon be over. What are you afraid of? A large black hole! It is empty, perhaps!"

Antony listens without saying anything in reply;—and, on the other side, appears another woman, marvellously young and beautiful. At first, he takes her for Ammonaria. But she is taller, fair as honey, rather plump, with paint on her cheeks, and roses on her head. Her long robe, covered with spangles, is studded with metallic mirrors. Her fleshly lips have a look of blood, and her somewhat heavy eyelashes are so much bathed in languor that one would imagine she was blind. She murmurs:

"Come, then, and enjoy yourself. Solomon recommends pleasure. Go where your heart leads you, and according to the desire of your eyes."

Antony—"To find what pleasure? My heart is sick; my eyes are dim!"

She replies:

"Hasten to the suburb of Racotis; push open a door painted blue; and, when you are in the atrium, where a jet of water is gurgling, a woman will present herself—in a peplum of white silk edged with gold, her hair dishevelled, and her laugh like sounds made by rattlesnakes. She is clever. In her caress you will taste the pride of an initiation, and the satisfaction of a want. Have you pressed against your bosom a maiden who loved you? Recall to your mind her remorse, which vanished under a flood of sweet tears. You can imagine yourself—can you not?—walking through the woods beneath the light of the moon. At the pressure of your hands joined with hers a shudder runs through both of you; your eyes, brought close together, overflow from one to the other like immaterial waves, and your heart is full; it is bursting; it is a delicious whirlwind, an overpowering intoxication."

The old woman—"You need not experience joys to feel their bitterness! You need only see them from afar, and disgust takes

136

possession of you. You must needs be wearied with the monotony of the same actions, the duration of the days, the ugliness of the world, and the stupidity of the sun!"

Antony—"Oh! yes; all that it shines upon is displeasing to me."

The young woman—"Hermit! hermit! you shall find diamonds among the pebbles, fountains beneath the sand, a delight in the dangers which you despise; and there are even places on the earth so beautiful that you are filled with a longing to embrace them."

The old woman—"Every evening when you lie down to sleep on the earth, you hope that it may soon cover you."

The young woman—"Nevertheless, you believe in the resurrection of the flesh, which is the transport of life into eternity."

The old woman, while speaking, has been growing more emaciated, and, above her skull, which has no hair upon it, a bat has been making circles in the air.

The young woman has become plumper. Her robe changes colour; her nostrils swell; her eyes roll softly.

The first says, opening her arms:

"Come! I am consolation, rest, oblivion, eternal peace!"

And the second offering her breast:

"I am the soother, the joy, the life, the happiness inexhaustible!"

Antony turns on his heel to fly. Each of them places a hand upon his shoulder.

The winding-sheet flies open, and reveals the skeleton of Death. The robe bursts open, and presents to view the entire body of Lust, which has a slender figure, with an enormous development behind, and great, undulating masses of hair, disappearing towards the end.

Antony remains motionless between the pair, contemplating them.

Death says to him—

"This moment, or a little later—what does it matter? You belong to me, like the suns, the nations, the cities, the kings, the snow on the mountains, and the grass in the fields. I fly higher than the sparrow-hawk, I run more quickly than the gazelle; I keep pace even with hope; I have conquered God!"

Lust—"Do not resist; I am omnipotent. The forests echo with my sighs; the waves are stirred by my agitations. Virtue, courage, piety, are dissolved in the perfume of my breath. I accompany man at every step he takes; and on the threshold of the tomb he comes back to me."

Death—"I will reveal to you what you tried to grasp by the light of torches on the features of the dead—or when you rambled beyond the Pyramids in those vast sand-heaps composed of human remains. From time to time, a piece of skull rolled under your sandal. You took it out of the dust; you made it slip between your fingers; and your mind, becoming absorbed in it, was plunged into nothingness."

Lust—"Mine is a deeper gulf! Marble slabs have inspired impure loves. People rush towards meetings that terrify them, and rivet the very chains which they curse. Whence comes the witchery of courtesans, the extravagance of dreams, the immensity of my sadness?"

Death—"My irony surpasses that of all other things. There are convulsions of joy at the funerals of kings and at the extermination of peoples; and they make war with music, plumes, flags, golden harnesses, and a display of ceremony to pay me the greater homage."

Lust—"My anger is as strong as yours. I howl, I bite, I have sweats of agony, and corpse-like appearances."

138

Death—"It is I who make you serious; let us embrace each other!"

Death chuckles; Lust roars. They seize each other's figures, and sing together:

"I hasten the dissolution of matter."

"I facilitate the scattering of germs!"

"Thou destroyest that I may renew!"

"Thou engenderest that I may destroy!"

"Active my power!"

"Fruitful my decay!"

And their voices, whose echoes, rolling forth, fill the horizon, become so powerful that Antony falls backward.

A shock, from time to time, causes him to half open his eyes; and he perceives, in the midst of the darkness, a kind of monster before him.

It is a death's-head with a crown of roses. It rises above the torso of a woman white as mother-of-pearl. Beneath, a winding-sheet, starred with points of gold, makes a kind of train;—and the entire body undulates, like a gigantic worm holding itself erect.

The vision grows fainter, and then fades away.

Antony, rises again—"This time, once more, it was the Devil, and under his two-fold aspect—the spirit of voluptuousness and the spirit of destruction. Neither terrifies me. I thrust happiness aside, and feel that I am eternal.

"Thus, death is only an illusion, a veil, masking at certain points the continuity of life. But substance, being one, why is there a variety of forms? There must be somewhere primordial figures, whose bodies are only images. If one could see, one would know the bond between mind and matter, wherein Being consists!

139

"There are those figures which were painted at Babylon on the wall of the temple of Belus, and they covered a mosaic in the port of Carthage. I, myself, have sometimes seen in the sky what seemed like forms of spirits. Those who traverse the desert meet animals passing all conception ..."

And, opposite him, on the other side of the Nile, lo! the Sphinx appears.

It stretches out its feet, shakes the fillets on its forehead, and lies down upon its belly.

Jumping, flying, spirting fire through its nostrils, and striking its wings with its dragon's tail, the Chimera with its green eyes, winds round, and barks. The curls of its head, thrown back on one side, intermingle with the hair on its haunches; and on the other side they hang over the sand, and move to and fro with the swaying of its entire body.

The Sphinx is motionless, and gazes at the Chimera:

"Here, Chimera; stop!"

The Chimera—"No, never!"

The Sphinx—"Do not run so quickly; do not fly so high; do not bark so loud!"

The Chimera—"Do not address me, do not address me any more, since you remain forever silent!"

The Sphinx—"Cease casting your flames in my face and flinging your yells in my ears; you shall not melt my granite!"

The Chimera—"You will not get hold of me, terrible Sphinx!"

The Sphinx—"You are too foolish to live with me!"

The Chimera—"You are too clumsy to follow me!"

The Sphinx—"And where are you going that you run so quickly?"

The Chimera—"I gallop into the corridors of the labyrinth; I hover over the mountains; I skim along the waves; I yelp at the bottoms of precipices; I hang by my jaws on the skirts of the clouds. With my trailing tail I scratch the coasts, and the hills have taken their curb according to the form of my shoulders. But as for you, I find you perpetually motionless; or, rather, with the end of your claw tracing letters on the sand."

The Sphinx—"That is because I keep my secret! I reflect and I calculate. The sea returns to its bed; the blades of corn balance themselves in the wind; the caravans pass; the dust flies off; the cities crumble;—but my glance, which nothing can turn aside, remains concentrated on the objects which cover an inaccessible horizon."

The Chimera—"As for me, I am light and joyous! I discover in men dazzling perspectives, with Paradises in the clouds and distant felicities. I pour into their souls the eternal insanities, projects of happiness, plans for the future, dreams of glory, and oaths of love, as well as virtuous resolutions. I drive them on perilous voyages and on mighty enterprises. I have carved with my claws the marvels of architecture. It is I that hung the little bells on the tomb of Porsenna, and surrounded with a wall of Corinthian brass the quays of the Atlantides.

"I seek fresh perfumes, larger flowers, pleasures hitherto unknown. If anywhere I find a man whose soul reposes in wisdom, I fall upon him and strangle him."

The Sphinx—"All those whom the desire of God torments, I have devoured.

"The strongest, in order to climb to my royal forehead, mount upon the stripes of my fillets as on the steps of a staircase. Weariness takes possession of them, and they fall back of their own accord."

Antony begins to tremble. He is not before his cell, but in the desert, having at either side of him those two monstrous animals, whose jaws graze his shoulders.

The Sphinx—"O Fantasy, bear me on thy wings to enliven thy sadness!"

The Chimera—"O Unknown One, I am in love with thine eyes! I turn round thee, soliciting allayment of that which devours me!"

The Sphinx—"My feet cannot raise themselves. The lichen, like a ringworm, has grown over my mouth. By dint of thinking, I have no longer anything to say."

The Chimera—"You lie, hypocritical Sphinx! How is it that you are always addressing me and abjuring me?"

The Sphinx—"It is you, unmanageable caprice, who pass and whirl about."

The Chimera—"Is that my fault? Come, now, just let me be!"

It barks.

The Sphinx—"You move away; you avoid me!"

The Sphinx grumbles.

The Chimera—"Let us make the attempt! You crush me!"

The Sphinx—"No; impossible!"

And sinking, little by little, it disappears in the sand, while the Chimera, crawling, with its tongue out, departs with a winding movement.

The breath issuing from its mouth has produced a fog.

In this fog Antony traces masses of clouds and imperfect curves. Finally, he distinguishes what appear to be human bodies.

And first advances the group of Astomi, like air-balls passing across the sun.

"Don't puff too strongly! The drops of rain bruise us; the false sounds excoriate us; the darkness blinds us. Composed of breezes and of perfumes, we roll, we float—a little more than dreams, not entirely beings."

The Nisnas have but one eye, one cheek, one hand, one leg, half a body, and half a heart. And they say, in a very loud tone:

"We live quite at our ease in our halves of houses with our halves of wives and our halves of children."

The Blemmyes, absolutely bereft of heads—

"Our shoulders are the largest;—and there is not an ox, a rhinoceros, or an elephant that is capable of carrying what we carry.

"Arrows, and a sort of vague outline are imprinted on our breasts—that is all! We reduce digestion to thought; we subtilise secretions. For us God floats peacefully in the internal chyle.

"We proceed straight on our way, passing through every mire, running along the verge of every abyss; and we are the most industrious, happy, and virtuous people."

The Pygmies—"Little good-fellows, we swarm over the world, like vermin on the hump of a dromedary.

"We are burnt, drowned, or run over; but we always reappear more full of life and more numerous—terrible from the multitude of us that exists!"

The Sciapodes—"Kept on the ground by our flowing locks, long as creeping plants, we vegetate under the shelter of our feet, which are as large as parasols; and the light reaches us through the spaces between our wide heels. No disorder and no toil! To keep the head as low as possible—that is the secret of happiness!"

Their lifted thighs, resembling trunks of trees, increase in number. And now a forest appears in which huge apes rush along on four paws. They are men with dogs' heads.

The Cynocephali—"We leap from branch to branch to suck the eggs, and we pluck the little birds; then we put their nests upon our heads after the fashion of caps.

"We do not fail to snatch away the worst of the cows, and we destroy the lynxes' eyes. Tearing the flowers, crushing the fruits, agitating the springs, we are the masters—by the strength of our arms and the fierceness of our hearts.

"Be bold, comrades, and snap your jaws!"

Blood and milk flow from their lips. The rain streams over their hairy backs.

Antony inhales the freshness of green leaves which are agitated as the branches of the trees dash against each other. All at once appears a large black stag with a bull's head, carrying between his two ears a mass of white horns.

The Sadhuzag—"My seventy-four antlers are hollow like flutes. When I turn myself towards the south wind, sounds go forth from them that draw around me the ravished beasts. The serpents come winding to my feet; the wasps stick in my nostrils; and the parrots, the doves, and the ibises alight upon my branches. Listen!"

He bends back his horns, from which issues an unutterably sweet music.

Antony presses both his hands above his heart. It seems to him as if this melody were about to carry off his soul.

The Sadhuzag—"But, when I turn towards the north wind, my horns, more bushy than a battalion of spears, emit a howling noise. The forests thrill; the rivers swell; the husks of the fruit burst, and blades of grass stand erect like a coward's hair. Listen!"

He bows down his branches, from which now come forth discordant cries. Antony feels as if he were torn asunder, and his horror is increased on seeing the Mantichor, a gigantic red lion with a human figure and three rows of teeth:

"The silky texture of my scarlet hair mingles with the yellowness of the sands. I breathe through my nostrils the terror of solitudes. I spit forth the plague. I devour armies when they venture into the desert. My nails are twisted like gimlets; my teeth are cut like a saw; and my hair, wriggled out of shape, bristles with darts which I scatter, right and left, behind me. Hold! hold!"

The Mantichor casts thorns from his tail, which radiate, like arrows, in all directions. Drops of blood flow, spattering over the foliage.

The Catoblepas appears, a black buffalo, with a pig's head hanging to the earth, and connected with his shoulders by a slender neck, long and flabby as an empty gut. He is wallowing on the ground; and his feet disappear under the enormous mane of hard hairs that descend over his face:

"Fat, melancholy, savage, I remain continually feeling the mire under my stomach. My skull is so heavy that it is impossible for me to carry it. I roll it around slowly; and, opening my jaws, I snatch with my tongue the poisonous herbs that are moistened with my breath. I once devoured my paws without noticing it.

"No one, Antony, has ever seen my eyes, or those who have seen them are dead. If I but raised my eyelids—my eyelids red and swollen—that instant you would die."

Antony—"Oh! that thing! ... Well! well! As if I had any such longing! Its stupidity attracts me. No! no! I will not!" He looks fixedly on the ground. But the grass lights up, and, in the twistings of the flames, stands erect the Basilisk, a huge, violet serpent, with a trilobate crest and two teeth—one above, the other below:

"Take care! You are about to fall into my jaws! I drink fire. I am fire myself; and from every quarter I suck it in—from clouds, from pebbles, from dead trees, from the hair of animals, and from the surface of marshes. My temperature supports the volcanoes. I cause the lustre of precious stones and the colour of metals."

The Griffin, a lion with a vulture's beak, white wings, red paws, and blue neck—"I am the master of the profound splendours. I know the secret of the tombs where the old kings sleep. A chain, which issues from the wall, keeps their heads erect. Near them, in basins of porphyry, women whom they have loved float upon black liquids. Their treasures are ranged in halls, in lozenges, in hillocks, and in pyramids; and, lower, far below the tombs, after long journeys in the midst of suffocating darkness, are rivers of gold with forests of diamonds, meadows of carbuncles, and lakes of quicksilver. With my back against the door of the vault, and my claws in the air, I watch with my flaming eyes those who may think fit to come there. The immense plain, even to the furthest point of the horizon, is quite bare and whitened with travellers' bones. For you the bronze doors will open, and you will inhale the vapour of the mines; you will descend into the caverns ... Quick! quick!"

He digs the earth with his claws, crowing like a cock.

A thousand voices reply to him. The forest trembles.

And all sorts of horrible beasts arise: the Tragelaphus, half-stag, half-ox; the Myrmecoleo, a lion in front, an ant behind, whose genitals are turned backwards; the python, Aksar, of sixty cubits, who frightened Moses; the great weasel, Pastinaca, which kills trees by its odour; the Presteros, which renders idiotic those who touch it; the Mirag, a horned hare dwelling in the islands of the sea. The Copard Phalmant bursts his belly by dint of howling; the Senad, a bear with three heads, tears its little ones with its mouth; the dog, Cepus, scatters on the rocks the blue milk of its dugs. Mosquitoes begin to buzz, toads to jump, and serpents to hiss. Lightnings flash; down comes the hail.

Then there are squalls, which reveal anatomical marvels. There are alligators' heads with roebucks' feet, owls with serpents' tails, swine with tigers' muzzles, goats with asses' rumps, frogs covered with hair like bears, chameleons large as hippopotami, calves with two heads, one of which weeps while the other bellows, four f[oe]tuses holding each other by the navel and spinning like tops, and winged bellies which flutter like gnats.

146

They rain down from the sky; they spring out of the ground; they glide from the rocks. Everywhere eyes flash, mouths roar; the breasts bulge out; the claws lengthen; the teeth gnash; the flesh quivers. Some of them bring forth their young; others with a single bite, devour one another.

Suffocating from their very numbers, multiplying by their contact, they climb on top of one another; and they all keep stirring about Antony with a regular swaying motion, as if the soil were the deck of a vessel.

He feels close to his calves the trailing of slugs, and on his hands the cold touch of vipers; and spiders spinning their webs enclose him in their network.

But the circle of monsters begins to open; the sky suddenly becomes blue, and the unicorn makes its appearance:

"Off I gallop! Off I gallop!

"I have hoofs of ivory, teeth of steel, a head coloured purple, a body like snow, and the horn on my forehead has the varied hues of the rainbow.

"I travel from Chaldea to the Tartar desert, on the banks of the Ganges, and into Mesopotamia. I outstrip the ostriches. I run so rapidly that I draw the wind along with me. I rub my back against the palm-trees; I roll myself in the bamboos. With one bound I jump across the rivers. Doves fly above my head. Only a virgin can bridle me.

"Off I gallop! Off I gallop!"

Antony watches him flying away.

And, keeping his eyes still raised, he perceives all the birds that are nourished by the wind: the Gouith, the Ahuti, the Alphalim, the Jukneth from the mountains of Caff, and the Homaï of the Arabs, which are the souls of murdered men. He hears the parrots utter human speech, then the great web-footed Pelasgians, who sob like children or chuckle like old women.

A briny breath of air strikes his nostrils. A seashore is now before him.

At a distance rise waterspouts, lashed up by the whales; and at the extremity of the horizon the beasts of the sea, round, like leather bottles, flat, like strips of metal, or indented, like saws, advance, crawling over the sand:

"You are about to come with us into our unfathomable depths, never penetrated by man before. Different races dwell in the country of the ocean. Some are in the abode of the tempests; others swim openly in the transparency of the cold waves, browse like oxen over the coral plains, sniff in with their nostrils the ebbing tide, or carry on their shoulders the weight of the ocean-springs."

Phosphorescences flash from the hairs of the seals and from the scales of the fishes. Sea-hedgehogs turn around like wheels; Ammon's horns unroll themselves like cables; oysters make sounds with the fastenings of their shells; polypi spread out their tentacles; medusæ quiver like crystal balls; sponges float; anemones squirt out water; and mosses and seaweed shoot up.

And all kinds of plants spread out into branches, twist themselves into tendrils, lengthen into points, and grow round like fans. Pumpkins present the appearance of bosoms, and creeping plants entwine themselves like serpents.

The Dedaims of Babylon, which are trees, have as their fruits human heads; mandrakes sing; and the root Baaras runs into the grass.

And now the plants can no longer be distinguished from the animals. Polyparies, which have the appearance of sycamores, carry arms on their branches. Antony fancies he can trace a caterpillar between two leaves; it is a butterfly which flits away. He is on the

148

point of walking over some shingle when up springs a grey grasshopper. Insects, like petals of roses, garnish a bush; the remains of ephemera make a bed of snow upon the soil.

And, next, the plants are indistinguishable from the stones.

Pebbles bear a resemblance to brains, stalactites to udders, and iron-dust to tapestries adorned with figures. In pieces of ice he can trace efflorescences, impressions of bushes and shells—so that one cannot tell whether they are the impressions of those objects or the objects themselves. Diamonds glisten like eyes, and minerals palpitate.

And he is no longer afraid! He lies down flat on his face, resting on his two elbows, and, holding in his breath, he gazes around.

Insects without stomachs keep eating; dried-up ferns begin to bloom afresh; and limbs which were wanting sprout forth again.

Finally, he perceives little globular bodies as large as pins' heads, and garnished all round with eyelashes. A vibration agitates them.

Antony, in ecstasy—

"O bliss! bliss! I have seen the birth of life; I have seen the beginning of motion. The blood beats so strongly in my veins that it seems about to burst them. I feel a longing to fly, to swim, to bark, to bellow, to howl. I would like to have wings, a tortoise-shell, a rind, to blow out smoke, to wear a trunk, to twist my body, to spread myself everywhere, to be in everything, to emanate with odours, to grow like plants, to flow like water, to vibrate like sound, to shine like light, to be outlined on every form, to penetrate every atom, to descend to the very depths of matter—to be matter!"

The dawn appears at last; and, like the uplifted curtains of a tabernacle, golden clouds, wreathing themselves into large volutes, reveal the sky.

In the very middle of it, and in the disc of the sun itself, shines the face of Jesus Christ.

149